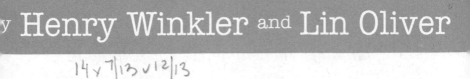

by Henry Winkler and Lin Oliver

14 x 7/13 ✓12/13

HANK ZIPZER

The World's Greatest Underachiever

My Secret Life as a Ping-Pong Wizard

Grosset & Dunlap

Master Zipzer and I deeply appreciate the fabulous "Penguinettes" for helping to introduce us to millions of readers: Bonnie Bader, Mariann Donato, Jess Michaels, Shane Breaux, Katrina Weidknecht, Gina Maolucci, Angela Jones, Lucy Del Priore, and Lara Phan. And always, to Stacey—H.W.

For Theo, my beloved first son and wizard of many fine arts, including Ping-Pong—L.O.

Cover illustration by Carol Heyer

GROSSET & DUNLAP
Published by the Penguin Group
Penguin Group (USA) Inc., 375 Hudson Street, New York, New York 10014, U.S.A.
Penguin Group (Canada), 10 Alcorn Avenue, Toronto, Ontario, Canada M4V 3B2
(a division of Pearson Penguin Canada Inc.)
Penguin Books Ltd, 80 Strand, London WC2R 0RL, England
Penguin Ireland, 25 St Stephen's Green, Dublin 2, Ireland
(a division of Penguin Books Ltd)
Penguin Group (Australia), 250 Camberwell Road, Camberwell,
Victoria 3124, Australia (a division of Pearson Australia Group Pty Ltd)
Penguin Books India Pvt Ltd, 11 Community Centre, Panchsheel Park,
New Delhi - 110 017, India
Penguin Group (NZ), Cnr Airborne and Rosedale Roads, Albany, Auckland 1310,
New Zealand (a division of Pearson New Zealand Ltd)
Penguin Books (South Africa) (Pty) Ltd, 24 Sturdee Avenue,
Rosebank, Johannesburg 2196, South Africa

Penguin Books Ltd, Registered Offices:
80 Strand, London WC2R 0RL, England

Library of Congress Control Number: 2005015144

ISBN 0-448-43749-X (pbk)   10 9 8 7 6 5 4 3 2 1
ISBN 0-448-43877-1 (hc)   10 9 8 7 6 5 4 3 2 1

CHAPTER 1

"THIS IS IT, ZIP," my best friend Frankie Townsend said as we slid into our seats in Room 31, our new classroom on the third floor. "The first day of fifth grade. Let's kick it off with a bang."

No sooner were those words out of his mouth than we heard a huge *BANG* in our classroom!

Correction. It wasn't exactly a bang. It was a screeching buzz followed by a loud crackle topped off with a high-pitched squeak that sent goose bumps down to the backs of my knees.

I looked around the classroom to see where the knee-bumping noise was coming from. It took me a second to realize that it was the loudspeaker above the door, screeching like it had just gotten a humongous booster shot at the doctor. I had to do something about that sound.

Quickly, I tore off the corner of a sheet of paper from my new spiral notebook, popped the paper into my mouth, and rolled it into a ball with my tongue. Then I blew with all my might and shot that spitball right at the center of the loudspeaker.

Bull's-eye! Hank Zipzer, you and your mouth have one great aim.

"Nice shot, dude," Luke Whitman cheered, putting up his hand to slap me a high five. As my hand made contact with his, I noticed that his palm was crusted with a lot of brown gooky stuff, but I high-fived him anyway.

"Check out your hang time," Frankie said, pointing to my spitball, which was still clinging to the center of the loudspeaker.

I don't mean to brag about my saliva, but that spitball hung on for a good ten seconds before it dropped to the floor. When it did, Luke Whitman held up his hand to slap me another high five. This time, I hesitated because of the already mentioned crusty palm situation.

"Don't worry, it's just oatmeal," Luke said. "The snail slime makes it hard to get off."

If you knew Luke, you'd understand. He likes bugs and snails. And he doesn't like to wash his hands. Enough said.

"Both of you boys are completely and totally disgusting," said Joelle Adwin, who had just sat down in the desk across the aisle from me.

Oh no, I have Joelle Adwin in my class!

Joelle is the expert in completely and totally disgusting boys, since her boyfriend is the king of them all. She has the honor of being the girlfriend of the completely and totally disgusting Nick "The Tick" McKelty, who wears his already-been-chewed breakfast in between his two front teeth and snorts like a hippo when he laughs.

Just then, McKelty walked into class.

Double oh-no with a cherry on top! McKelty's in my class too. Is this bad luck or what?

Nick took his seat across from Joelle and turned to me to see what trouble he could cause. This morning he was wearing raisin toast and I think raspberry jam in between his teeth.

"You suck, Zipzer," he said. That's McKelty's special way of saying hello to me.

I turned my back on him, which is my special way of saying hello to him. My other best friend, Ashley Wong, had just taken the seat next to Frankie. At least my two best friends were in my class again this year.

"I hate to say this, Hank, but Joelle does have a point," Ashley whispered. She pointed to the spitball lying on the floor under the loudspeaker. "You should pick it up."

I slipped out of my desk, crouched over to where the spitball was still lying on the floor, and scooped it up. Suddenly, the loudspeaker started to crackle again, only this time, the crackling turned into a voice.

"This is your principal, Leland Love, speaking," blared the loudspeaker. "Welcome to a new school year at PS 87."

Still in my crouch, I tossed the spitball over to the wastebasket next to the teacher's desk. Oops, it missed and landed on the floor.

"Students in Room 31 should take their seats—and that goes especially for you, Hank Zipzer," Principal Love said.

How did he know I was out of my seat? Does the loudspeaker have eyes?

"Any of you who are acting up or shooting spitballs will have to report directly to my office. Did you hear me, Hank Zipzer?"

Spitballs! How did he know I was shooting spitballs? Maybe his eyes had come out of their sockets, jumped from his head, and rolled up and down the hall to spy on kids.

I hadn't heard Principal Love's voice in almost a month, since summer school ended. I'd like to say I missed hearing it. But it wouldn't be true. Not even a little teeny bit.

"Students in Room 31, I have received a message from your teacher," Principal Love went on. "She has telephoned to say she will be a few minutes late due to a detained bus on Broadway. You are to stay in your seats until she arrives. And that goes especially for you—"

The whole class joined in with the loudspeaker to finish the sentence. "Hank Zipzer," they chanted in unison.

The leader of this chant was Ramon Perez. I'd never even been in a class with him before. How did he know that I always get in trouble? Well, to be fair to Ramon, I guess I do have a reputation for getting in trouble with the principal. I try very hard not to break the rules, but sometimes I just can't stop myself from bending them really hard.

There was another blast of that screeching sound, then the loudspeaker clicked off.

Everybody started to talk at once. We were dying to know who our new teacher was going to be.

"I heard she's beautiful," Ryan Shimozato said.

"Like a beauty queen or something?" Matthew "I'm not too swift" Barbarosa asked. *Hey, where is his best friend, Salvatore Mendez? He must have been put in the other fifth-grade room. Man, I'd hate to be separated from Frankie and Ashley.*

"I'll bet she was Miss Alabama," Nick McKelty said in his big, loud voice.

"Why Alabama?" Frankie asked him.

"It's the only state I could think of," McKelty said, and shrugged. Everyone burst out laughing, and his face turned bright red.

"What's so funny?" he shouted. "I know all the other forty states. I just don't feel like saying them now."

Joelle reached over and patted McKelty's arm.

"There are fifty states, Nicky," I could hear her whisper.

"I knew that," he snapped back at her. "I wanted to see if you did."

McKelty can never admit when he's wrong, which, by the way, he is most of the time. I don't know why anyone, even Joelle Adwin who loves her cell phone so much that she wants to marry it, would want to be his girlfriend.

"I just hope the new teacher is nice," Ashley said, adjusting her baseball hat, which she had decorated with red rhinestones that said 5th GRADE ROCKS! on the bill.

"You said it, Ashweena," Frankie nodded. "Not like a certain Ms. Adolf."

Ms. Adolf was our fourth-grade teacher and she specialized in the No-Fun, No-Laughing, Sit-Still, Give-Lots-of-Homework kind of teaching. She wore all-grey clothes every single day, to match her grey hair and grey glasses and grey face.

Just that morning, Frankie and Ashley and I had just been talking on the way to school about how glad we were to be in the fifth grade and leave Ms. Adolf to the fourth-graders. My sister, Emily the Perfect, and her boyfriend, Robert Upchurch the Know-It-All, were in the fourth grade this year. I wondered if they were sitting in Ms. Adolf's class right that very minute.

Oh yeah, that thought makes me smile.

"Footsteps!" a new kid named Marcus called out.

"Here she comes," everyone whispered.

We all sat up straight in our desks and looked toward the door. The footsteps got louder and louder as they got closer and closer. I could feel my heart beating a little faster. That may sound silly, but I couldn't wait to see who my teacher was. It was a big moment. When you think about it, you spend more time with your teacher than you do with your mom and dad. I mean, six hours a day, five days a week, that makes . . . let me see now . . . oh forget it, I'm terrible at math.

I looked toward the door and could see the new teacher through the frosty glass window. I couldn't see a face, just an outline.

No one said a word as the doorknob turned. Slowly, slowly, the door opened. There she was.

"Hello, pupils," she said. "I'm your fifth-grade teacher!"

CHAPTER 2

IT WAS MS. ADOLF!
No, I'm not kidding. I wish I were.
But I'm not.

CHAPTER 3

TEN THINGS ANY NORMAL KID WOULD SAY WHEN HE FINDS OUT HE HAS MS. ADOLF AGAIN

1. I'm dead.
2. I'm dead meat.
3. I'm dead rat meat.
4. I'm double-dead rat meat.
5. I'm double-dead rat meat with only one claw.
6. Wait a minute. Let me rub my eyes and check again, because maybe what I'm seeing isn't real.
7. Nope, it's her. Ms. Adolf in the flesh.
8. You can handle this, Hank. It's only a year.
9. That's 365 days.

10. Let me get out my calculator. That is 8,760 hours. 525,600 minutes. 31,536,000 seconds.
11. I'm going to spend the next 31 million seconds with Ms. Adolf.
12. Oh, yeah. I'm rat meat times 31 million.
13. Stick a fork in me. I'm done.*

*I know, I know. This is more than ten things. But give me a break, will you? If you just found out that you had Ms. Adolf again, you wouldn't be able to count, either.

CHAPTER 4

Ms. ADOLF MARCHED right to her desk and unlocked the top drawer with a key she wears on a lanyard around her neck. She reached in the drawer, pulled out a navy blue roll book, and began calling roll. As each student said "here," she made what she thought was a welcoming comment.

Let me just say this: Her comments weren't exactly welcoming. She could have said, "Hey, great to see you, kids. Did you have a terrific summer?"

Nope. That's not the Ms. Adolf we know and don't love. Here's what she said instead.

To Ryan Shimozato, she said, "Spit out your gum and leave the rest of the pack with me."

And to Ashley, she said, "No hats in class, Ms. Wong. You know that."

To Luke Whitman, she said, "Go to the

restroom immediately and wash your hands." Actually, that wasn't such a bad idea.

To Joelle Adwin, she said, "If I see that cell phone again, young lady, I'll take it away for good."

And to Frankie, who is a perfect student, she said, "Sit up straight, Mr. Townsend. You are in school, not in your living room."

Even the new kid, Marcus, didn't get a "nice to have you with us." Instead she told him his transfer paperwork was not in order.

Way to make the new guy feel good, Ms. A.

When she called my name, which was last as usual because my name starts with a *Z* she took off her glasses and stared at me like I was a fly on her macaroni and cheese lunch.

"Mr. Zipzer, I hope we won't have a repeat of last year," she said.

"You and me both, Ms. Adolf," I said. "I'm going to try my best every day."

"Trying is not enough, Henry. I am looking for excellence."

"I'm looking for it too," I answered. "I just haven't found it."

Everyone started to laugh, which I wished

they wouldn't have, because kids laughing is one of the things that really makes Ms. Adolf mad.

"Fifth grade is no laughing matter," she said, putting down her roll book and strolling up and down the aisles. "It's not fun and games like fourth grade was."

Fun and games? Did I miss something? I don't remember any fun in the fourth grade, and the only games we ever played were spelling games, which don't exactly zoom to the top of my fun list.

"Fifth grade is serious business, and I expect you will all find it extremely challenging."

Challenging. That's teacher talk for really hard. Dr. Berger uses that word a lot. She is the learning specialist at my school who works with kids like me who have learning issues. She always tells me that reading is *challenging* for me. What she's saying is that it's harder for me than for a lot of other kids. I don't mind it when she says it, because she's trying to be nice. But when Ms. Adolf said that fifth grade was going to be *extremely challenging*, I minded it. It made those goose bumps pop up behind my knees again.

"Of course, we will have many pleasant times as well," Ms. Adolf went on as she circled the class and arrived back at the front. "For instance, I plan to have spelling bees every Friday."

Wow, get out the party hats. Here come the spelling games.

"And, of course, there's Math Bingo."

Toot the horns. Ring the bells. The excitement is almost too much!

"And we will have the occasional special event."

Wait a minute. A special event. That doesn't sound so bad. Maybe there'll be refreshments, like donuts and punch. That has possibilities.

"To start our schedule of special events, I'm happy to announce that the Parade of Athletes will be held in the gymnasium a week from Friday night."

"What's the Parade of Athletes?" Heather Payne asked. She was already taking notes. "I didn't see it on the master calendar when I was reviewing it last night."

Whoops. We were supposed to review the school calendar. I forgot. Come to think of it,

I forgot to take the master calendar home last June.

I wonder if it's still in my fourth-grade desk on the second floor. Maybe that piece of red licorice is still there too. I wonder if it's too hard to eat by now.

"The Parade of Athletes is a new school event to honor the many sports that people play," Ms. Adolf said, making it sound as much fun as a dentist appointment.

I put up my hand.

"Will there be punch and donuts?" I asked.

"The purpose of the evening is not to consume sugary foods that overstimulate the child," Ms. Adolf said. "The purpose is to have those of you who participate in sports demonstrate your skills."

"I'm going to show everyone my ace soccer moves," McKelty blurted out. "I was All City last year. The mayor of New York gave me his own personal congratulations."

Ashley and Frankie rolled their eyes at me. There it was on the very first day of school: the McKelty Factor. Truth times one hundred. First of all, McKelty is a world-class klutz. And second of all, the mayor of New York City doesn't even know he exists.

"Everyone is encouraged to join in the fun," Ms. Adolf said. "I, for one, am looking forward to participating."

Ms. Adolf? An athlete? What would she demonstrate? Grading papers?

"What sport do you play?" Ashley asked.

"I am a fencer," Ms. Adolf said. "I happen to be extremely skillful with the foil and saber."

Ms. Adolf suddenly picked up the stick that she uses to point out the right answers on the overhead projector. *"En garde,"* she shouted and, using the pointer like a sword, she lunged at the classroom door! I swear, if she had been wearing green tights, you would have thought she was Robin Hood.

Just as she lunged at the door, it swung open and Mr. Rock, our really cool music teacher who was also my summer school teacher, came in.

"Whoa, Fanny!" he screamed. "Where are you going with that thing?"

"I was demonstrating my thrust and parry," Ms. Adolf said. "I got carried away."

"It's good to get carried away," Mr. Rock

said with a laugh. "Don't you think so, kids?"

Ms. Adolf put down the stick, and tucked a few loose strands of her grey hair up into the bun that she wears on top of her head. "Don't encourage them," she said to him. "Now how can I help you, Mr. Rock?"

"I just wanted to make an announcement about soccer tryouts tomorrow," he said. "Everybody who wants to play can come out to the Sheep Meadow in Central Park after school. The volunteer soccer coaches will be there to check out your skills and put you on a team."

Mr. Rock is such a nice guy, he always winks at kids in the hall for no reason at all.

"Thank you, Mr. Rock," Ms. Adolf said. "And now, if you don't mind, we have work to do."

"Far be it from me to get in the way of work," he said. Just before he reached the hall, he stopped and said to all of us, "By the way, guys, we'll have punch and donuts."

Then he winked and walked out, leaving us there to face the year with the winkless, punchless, donutless Ms. Adolf.

CHAPTER 5

Ms. Adolf droned on for the longest two hours in the history of the human race. It was first-day-of-school stuff like how many lines our notebook paper had to have and how many sharpened number-two pencils had to be in our zipper bag at all times. There were also exciting details about how to make up homework assignments, and other things that are so boring that if I even mentioned them now, you'd close this book and never pick it up again.

When the recess bell rang, I felt like getting up and dancing for joy. In fact, I did. It wasn't a big-deal dance but just a little butt-shaking number that went along with a whooping sound.

"What are you doing, Zip Head?" McKelty said as he shoved by me and headed for the stairs. "It looks like you have a buzzing bee in your pants."

"I think he looks cute," Kim Paulson said. "Maybe you should demonstrate that dance at the Parade of Athletes, Hank."

Frankie gave me a friendly elbow in the ribs as we hurried down the three flights of stairs to the yard.

"You are aware, dude, that one of the finest girls in the class just called you cute," he pointed out, as if a thing like that needed any pointing out.

"Maybe there's hope for this year after all," I whispered.

We had barely reached the schoolyard when my sister, Emily, came running up to us, her braids flapping in the air like crow's wings.

"Hank! You're not going to believe it. We have the greatest fourth-grade teacher ever!" Emily said all in one gulp. "Her name is Ms. Andrews and she thinks it's fascinating that I love reptiles and she's really pretty too."

"Actually, she was a former Miss Alabama," Robert Upchurch chimed in. He follows Emily around like a shadow. A bony shadow with a white shirt and tie.

"We're going to do a gigantic unit on the tidal marshes of Alabama," Emily gushed on.

"With an emphasis on the life cycle of the brown water snake," Robert added.

"Man, some people get all the luck," Frankie said.

My sister Emily loves reptiles as much as Joelle Adwin loves her cell phone. You should see how Emily acts with Katherine, her pet iguana. She shares her secrets with her, and tells her how she understands her deep reptile feelings. Honestly, you'd think they were soul sisters, which come to think of it, they probably are. Emily's got a long snout and scaly skin, too.

"Bet you can't guess what other marsh creatures we're going to study," Emily continued on.

"Creatures that look like you, only they slither on their bellies." I smiled. I was happy with that little zinger.

"Fine, Hank. Be that way. I'm never going to tell you one thing about the courtship habits of swamp alligators, no matter how much you beg."

"Why don't we change the subject?" Ashley suggested.

"So who's your teacher?" Emily asked as we strolled out to the handball court in the middle of the yard.

"Don't ask, girlfriend," Frankie said.

"But I already did," Emily answered. She may be smart in the book area, but she's a little thick in the slang area.

"I'll give you a hint," I said, returning a red rubber ball to the little kids who were playing on the handball court. "Our teacher was supposed to be your teacher, until the world spun off its axis."

"Actually, the world could never fly off its axis," Robert said. "Because if it did, we would fall outside the gravitational pull of the sun and splinter off into space."

"Robert, doesn't it worry you that your mind is filled with this stuff?"

"Actually, it gives me a great sense of pride."

"It gives me a great sense of headache,"

Frankie laughed.

"I'll tell you who our teacher is, Emily," I said, seeing that she was getting frustrated with our joking around. "Our teacher is Ms. Adolf."

"No, she *was* your teacher. I'm talking about this year."

"We got her again," Ashley explained.

"Isn't that against the law?" Emily asked. "You can't have the same teacher twice."

"Which tells you everything you need to know about Ms. Adolf," Frankie said. "She's willing to break the law just to make our lives miserable."

"It's the pits," I said.

"Deep pits," Ashley sighed.

"Bottom of the bottom," Frankie added.

Emily reached into her pocket and pulled out a health-food granola bar. "Here, Hank. You can have my snack," she said. "You need it more than I do."

That's the thing about sisters. They're a total pain in the neck and then, just when you least expect it, they turn out to be really nice.

I was taking the wrapper off the granola bar when McKelty came charging up to me and grabbed the bar out of my hand. He stuck it in his oversized mouth and bit down with his scraggly teeth.

"What is this crud? It tastes like birdseed."

"It's a whole-grain oatmeal energy bar with flax and sunflower seeds," I told him.

McKelty handed what was left of the bar back to me. "Here, you eat it," he said. "You look like you need to bulk up before soccer try-outs tomorrow."

"You're not supposed to be bulky for soccer," Ashley told him. "You're supposed to be lean and mean."

"Trust me, McKelty," Frankie said. "Zip here has what it takes on the soccer field."

Frankie's a good friend, and he likes to say nice things about me. But I have to be honest with you. What he said was not true. Well, I am lean. And sometimes I'm mean, especially to Emily. But I definitely do not have what it takes on the soccer field. When I run down the field, I look like a wobbly old bike with loose wheels. But none of us—not Frankie, or Ashley or me—was about to share that sweet little picture with Nick McKelty.

Quite the opposite.

"Oh, I'll be at soccer tryouts, all right," I said. "No ball is safe around this foot."

Just as I lifted my foot to show it off to him, another big red rubber handball came flying off the court and landed accidentally on my shoe. I hadn't even seen it coming. Frankie gave me a look that said, "Don't act surprised, Zip. Be cool."

"Nice kick, Hankster," Ashley said.

I think McKelty was impressed, because he started to brag, which he always does when he's feeling like someone else might be better than he is.

"I'm going to be the first guy picked tomorrow," Nick the Tick said. "And not only that, I'm going to do the best soccer demonstration in the Parade of Athletes."

"Right, and my name is Bernice," Frankie fired back.

"Well hello, Bernice." McKelty grinned, thinking he had come up with a real clever comeback. He burst out laughing, and a spray of crumbs and seeds shot out at us through the gigantic space between his two front teeth. An aircraft carrier could sail right in between that gap.

Suddenly, a shrill whistle sounded right next to my ear. I wheeled around and was just about to say "Hey, what do you think you're doing?" when my mouth froze up mid-sentence. It was Ms. Adolf, holding a brand-new whistle she had added to the lanyard around her neck. It was grey. I ask you: Where in the world can a person even buy a grey whistle?

"Pupils, recess is officially over," she called out in her playground voice, which is strict like her regular voice, only louder. "It's time to get back to your desks so we can begin your fifth-grade studies."

"And that means you, Hank Zipzer," Principal Love said.

Principal Love? Where did he come from? And how'd he find me? That proves it. His eyeballs do come out and roll around school, just looking to get me in trouble.

I hadn't even started the fifth grade and already I was wondering if I'd ever even see the sixth grade.

CHAPTER 6

THE NEXT DAY, I spent the morning with the exciting, sweet, kind, loving, and always-has-a-good-word-for-me, Ms. Adolf. And to make things even more wonderful, we had a thrilling, action-packed, supercharged morning doing long division worksheets. She even threw in a few problems with the ever-popular decimal point.

I looked down at those sheets and all I could think of was the Hopi Indians. That might seem strange to you, but it wasn't to me. You see, the Hopi Indians wrote their whole history on the walls of their caves in a hieroglyphic code called pictographs. Ms. Adolf's long-division worksheets made about as much sense to me as those Hopi hieroglyphics. Actually, the cave paintings make more sense because sometimes you can see a buffalo or a warrior on a pony. What I had in front of me on my desk made my eyes spin in my sockets. They were going so fast, they were like propellers that were going to lift my butt right out of my seat. Thank goodness for the desktop that held me in place or I would have shot right through the ceiling.

At 10:14 that morning, Ms. Adolf said my second favorite word in the English language.

"Recess," she announced.

In case you're wondering what my first favorite word is, it's weekend. Except when I'm really hungry, and then it's pizza.

By the time I had walked down the stairs and through the double doors and out onto the playground, I was starting to feel happier.

Hank, think of your glass as half full rather than half empty.

That's what my grandpa, Papa Pete, always tells me. I always think of my glass as half full of chocolate milk, because I love chocolate milk, especially Nestlé Quik when you make it in a blender. We're talking smooth.

I looked around to decide how I was going to spend my fifteen minutes of recess. I saw

Frankie and Ashley pick up a soccer ball and start passing it to each other.

"Come on, Zip," Frankie called. "Dribble with us. We have to practice for tryouts later."

The truth was, I was nervous about the after-school tryouts. What if I didn't get picked for a team? I know, I know. That doesn't really happen because there are no cuts in this league. But what if I was the last one to get picked? That does happen. I'll bet you know someone it's happened to.

"No thanks," I hollered back to Frankie. "I'm in a dribble-free zone right now."

"Come on, Hank," Ashley said, kicking me the ball. "How are you going get better if you don't practice?"

"I'm going to think about that as I walk past the swings," I said. I kicked the ball back to her, and of course it went in totally the opposite direction. It landed right in front of Nick the Tick.

"Nice pass, soccer nerd," McKelty said. "I hope you don't get picked for my team."

McKelty was standing next to Joelle. They were standing close together, like boyfriend and girlfriend. I know the thought of McKelty even having a girlfriend is too icky to let into your mind, but sometimes the truth is hard to take.

"Nick tells me he's really good at soccer," Joelle said, looking up at him with her squinty little eyes. "He says he never misses the ball."

"Sure, if I had feet the size of tables, I wouldn't miss the ball either," I fired back.

I just have to take a minute and say that I do occasionally have great comebacks.

"Oh yeah, watch this," Nick said. He pulled back his big, thick leg at the end of which was his size-twelve Nike and let loose on the ball lying at his feet. I swear the ball said "ouch." It took off like a missile, flew across the yard, and landed smack in the middle of Ms. Adolf's backside. It was as if she had a soccer ball magnet under her grey skirt.

"Ooouuuph," she said, sounding like a wrestler who's just been pile-driven into the mat.

McKelty ran away, leaving me staring eyeball to eyeball at her.

"Henry, I think you owe me an apology."

"Ms. Adolf, I promise you I never touched

30

that ball. I'm allergic to that ball. That ball and I do not get along."

"Then perhaps you can explain how that ball hit me in the derriere."

I'm no rat, even when someone as obnoxious as Nick McKelty is involved.

"You're finding out what I already know. Soccer balls have minds of their own, Ms. Adolf."

Lucky for me that at that very moment, Luke Whitman thought it was necessary to show Katie Sperling his pet African centipede, Bugsy, which he had brought to school in a sandwich baggie.

"Gross!" Katie shrieked. "He's putting that hairy bug in my face!"

As Ms. Adolf turned to rescue Katie and put Bugsy back in his baggie, I took the opportunity to run as far away as I could, and ended up in the kindergarten area of the playground.

"Hi, Hank," said a little voice from the sandbox.

"Mason!" I said. "My man!"

Mason Harris Jerome Dunn is just about the cutest little kindergartner you'd ever want to see. I met him during summer school, and we became friends. He wears Donald Duck shirts every day. The guy is a Donald Duck nut and an artistic genius. No kidding. He drew a picture of the Brooklyn Bridge in the sand that looked so real, I wanted to walk across it and buy some Chinese dumplings at my favorite dumpling shop in Lower Manhattan.

"I'm not a man, Hank. I'm a kid."

"It's just an expression, my man. What are you drawing?"

"A pirate ship," he said.

"That's really cool. Want me to help you?"

"Uh-huh."

I picked up a stick and started to draw a cannon on the deck of Mason's ship. He was busy making a treasure chest. I hate to admit this— even to you—but I really love to play in the sand. No one there is counting your number-two pencils and telling you that fifth grade is serious business.

Suddenly, Mason got up.

"Now I'm going to play ball with Sam Chin."

"Hey, wait. Why are you leaving?"

"I'm practicing soccer for the Parade of All Feets."

"That's 'athletes,' dude."

"Okay. Bye, Hank."

Mason ran over to another little kindergarten guy who was holding a soccer ball. He kicked it to Mason, who stopped it with his foot.

"Want me to pass it to you, Hank?" Mason called to me.

"Sure, fire away," I said, getting up from the sandbox. This might be good practice for tryouts. I figured I'd be good enough to kick it back to a five-year-old.

Mason passed the soccer ball to me. It came straight and fast. He was good! I saw the ball coming and I put my foot out to stop it. I thought I had everything under control, but I missed it by a mile. The ball rolled right past me, bounced into the sandbox, and landed on the pirate ship.

"Wow, Mason, I'm sorry."

"That's okay, Hank. You'll learn."

This isn't a good sign for my tryouts later. I'm a full-fledged fifth-grader and I can't even stop a ball kicked by a kindergartner.

"Hey, guys, I've got an idea. Why don't you

play by yourselves for a while?"

"Do you have big-kid stuff to do?" Sam Chin said.

"You bet I do," I said. And I walked away trying to look like a big kid with somewhere to go.

Okay, Hank, so you don't want to play soccer with the fifth-graders. And you can't play soccer with the kindergartners. What's left?

You're not going to believe this, but those long-division worksheets were starting to look really good.

CHAPTER 7

THERE'S A SECTION OF CENTRAL PARK called the Sheep Meadow, which is a big, flat field just up from the carousel. Maybe you've heard about it. It's pretty famous because sometimes at night during the summer, they have concerts where tons of people crowd together to listen to music. I went there one time with my parents to see the Dave Matthews Band, but when Dave came out and started to play, everyone stood up and all I could see was a lot of adult rear ends. I think I'll wait until after I have a growth spurt or two until I go to a concert there again.

The soccer tryouts for all West-side kids were being held in Sheep Meadow. By the time we got there, there were hundreds of kids from many different schools all over the field. Ashley's mom had picked us up from school and walked us to the park, since my mom was at work in our deli, the Crunchy Pickle, and my dad had to take Emily to her allergist appointment. I was glad Ashley's mom took us, because she's a doctor and all she likes to do is sit on the bench and read articles about heart valves and skin rashes. She doesn't watch the tryouts, and she doesn't really care who's a good player and who's not.

Lots of different coaches were scattered around organizing how they were going to do their team tryouts. Mr. Rock had told Frankie and me to find Coach Gilroy. His son Patrick was in the fifth grade at Trinity School, and he was organizing a team for ten-to-eleven-year-old boys.

Mr. Rock said Coach Gilroy would be wearing a green and white jersey. I looked around the field and spotted him talking to a few of the dads.

I knew I was in trouble the minute I saw him. Coach Gilroy was a huge, muscular guy who was standing with his foot on one ball, and had three other balls tucked under his arm. He was a four-soccer-ball coach. All the other coaches on the field were holding just one. And listen to this: His soccer shorts were ironed with a crease down each leg. Who irons soccer shorts? Only a guy who's crazy-serious about his soccer, that's who.

Oh boy, Hank. Get your game face on. Yeah, I would if I knew where it was.

I have this thing about sports balls. They cause me lots and lots of problems. Except bowling balls. My grandfather, Papa Pete, is a champion bowler and he taught me his technique. On a good day, I can bowl two strikes in a row, which makes me feel unbelievably good. But other balls of the non-bowling type are really tricky. Last year, with a lot of help from Frankie and Papa Pete, I learned to pitch a softball. But that's all I can do. I mean, I can't field or hit or do any other softball-type stuff.

See, I love sports. I'm just not good at them. In my sessions with Dr. Berger, she has explained that a lot of kids with learning differences don't have good hand-eye coordination. That means that my eyes and my hands, or in this case my feet, are not talking to each other. Or if they are talking, they're not listening to each other very well.

"All right, players, take a knee," Coach Gilroy said in a big voice that sounded like

Darth Vader's. He had come over and gathered up about twenty of us guys. As we huddled together, I smelled something rotten, like a fish with bad breath.

Wait a minute. I know that smell. It's McKelty breath!

I looked around and, sure enough, there was Nick McKelty, taking a knee right next to me. First I had to get him in my class. And now he was on my soccer team. That was way too much McKelty time for me!

There was nothing to do about it, so I settled down on one knee and tried to look like I was comfortable in that position. All I kept thinking about was why you had to be on one knee. Wouldn't it be so much more comfortable to sit on your rump, which has built-in cushions? I guess it's because "All right, players, take a rump," doesn't sound very sporty.

"This is no-cut soccer," Coach Gilroy began, "so as of now, all you men are on the team. You're the Green Hornets. What are you?"

"Green Hornets!" everyone shouted. His son Patrick, a tall kid with bright blond hair, was shouting the loudest.

"I can't hear you," Coach Gilroy shouted back.

"Green Hornets!" we shouted even louder.

"What's the matter, cat got your tongue?"

"Green Hornets!" I shouted so loud, I thought my tonsils were going to fly out of my throat.

"That's more like it, men," Coach Gilroy said. "Now listen up and listen good. What we're going to do at tryouts is assess your skill level so I know how to play you. I'll be watching each of you very carefully."

I am not liking the sound of this. Truth time: I am hating the sound of this.

"Take a look around," the coach said. "See the red and black team? They're the Avengers. The gold and blue team? They're the Earthquakes. The orange and white team? They're the Thunder Clouds. We're here for one purpose and one purpose only: to beat them all. Are you with me?"

We all said yes.

"That was a wimpy yes, men."

"Yes, sir," we all shouted. Patrick was shouting so loud, his face was purple.

Wow, this Coach Gilroy was one tough guy. I wondered what it was like living at his house. Patrick probably has to do push-ups before dinner, march in a straight line to bed and, before he falls asleep, shout good night in a really loud, manly voice.

Coach Gilroy pointed at Frankie. "You, what's your name?"

"Frankie Townsend."

"Are you with me, Frankie Townsend?"

"I'm with ya all the way," Frankie answered. Oh man, that Frankie. He even sounded like an athlete.

"You," Coach Gilroy said, pointing his big, fleshy finger at me. "What's your name?"

"Hank Zipzer," I said. "With a Z. Actually with two Zs."

"This isn't a spelling contest, Zipzer. I'm here to know if you're with me. Now, are you?"

"Coach, if I were any more with you, I'd be attached to your shoe."

The other guys on the team started to laugh. I could hear Nick McKelty laughing louder than the rest, like a hippo snorting.

"There's always one," Coach Gilroy said.

"The funny guy. Okay, funny guy, let's see if you dribble as well as you joke. On your feet."

Before I could even stand up, he passed me the ball his left foot was resting on. It hit me on the outside of the ankle, which isn't exactly the first move you want to show your coach.

I looked down at that ball and desperately tried to make friends.

Come on, please, Mr. Ball. Just this once. Stick close to my foot.

There was a line of orange cones set up in front of us.

"All right, let me see you dribble that ball around each cone. Keep it sharp. Go!"

I froze. It was as though he had said "Stand still and don't move a muscle." If he had only said that, I would have been perfect. I stood there like one of the bronze statues in the park.

"Zip," I heard Frankie say. "Breathe. Oxygen is power."

I took a deep breath.

"Good, now dribble."

"Okay, Zipzer with a Z, what are you waiting for? The grass to grow?"

I took off, keeping the ball close to my feet by tapping it ever so lightly, first with one foot, then the other. I wanted to control the ball. The last thing I wanted was for the ball to take off without me.

Good, Hank. You're around the first cone. Okay, this isn't going so badly. Just slowly.

I was proud of myself. Apparently, Coach Gilroy wasn't.

"Could you go any slower, funny guy? The polar ice cap could melt by the time you've gotten around two cones."

The team laughed. I could hear McKelty laughing the loudest, naturally.

Don't look up, Hank. And don't listen. You need to concentrate. One foot, then the other. One cone, then the next. Focus. Concentrate.

All of a sudden I heard the blast of a whistle from somewhere across the field. Before I could stop my head, it had turned almost by itself, following the sound of the whistle. My feet, however, were moving in the opposite direction. *Bam!* I tripped over the ball, fell on the cone, and landed facedown in the grass. I was eye to eye with a line of ants carrying a leaf to their anthill. I wished I could join them. Carrying is something I can do.

"You've got to learn to focus, Zipzer," Coach Gilroy said.

"If I could, I would, sir," I said.

"Are you being a smart aleck?"

"No, sir. Focusing is one of my problems."

"Well, you'd better fix that if you want any playing time on this team," he said. "Now get over yourself, and get to the back of the line."

I was never so relieved to go to the back of the line. It was safe there.

"Who thinks he can show Zipzer how it's done?"

Of course, one hand shot up in the air. It was Nick McKelty's.

"What's your name?" Coach Gilroy asked him.

"Nick McKelty," he said. "But you can call me Striker. See this foot? It only knows how to kick goals."

"You've got a lot of confidence, McKelty."

"You would, too, if you were trained by the uncle of the first cousin of Brazil's soccer team's cook. I got connections, big-time."

"Good for you," Coach Gilroy said. "Let's see if you can connect your foot to the ball."

Nick the Tick placed the ball in between his size-twelve feet. He kicked the ball and took off toward the first cone, but instead of going around it, he knocked it down like a bowling pin.

"The object is to go around the cones, McKelty, not through them," Coach Gilroy shouted.

McKelty was as graceful as an elephant on ice skates. He knocked down every single cone, his big, floppy feet kicking up clumps of grass and mud as he went down the line. It was ugly. But, as usual, McKelty was proud of himself. The guy has no idea what a clodhopper he is.

"How'd you like that, Coach?" he grinned when he was finally finished.

"I didn't," Coach Gilroy said. "What do I have here? All the rejects from the girls' team?"

That was a nasty remark. I thought of Ashley and what a great soccer player she was. Coach Gilroy should only be so lucky to get a girl player like Ashley.

"Is there anyone who can handle a ball?" I heard him say.

Matthew Barbarosa raised his hand. "I volunteer Frankie Townsend," he said. "He's good at everything in and out of the classroom."

"I'll be the judge of that," Coach Gilroy said. "Hey, Zipzer, set up the cones so Townsend can take a try."

Set up the cones? Oh yeah, now there's something I can do. And I can do it fast too.

Frankie got up and bent over to touch his toes, which is all he needs to do to warm up. Coach Gilroy tossed him a ball, which Frankie caught on his knee and let drop in between his feet. With almost no effort at all, he dribbled the ball in and out of the orange cones, making sharp little turns and keeping low to the ground. When he reached the last cone, he turned the ball around and came back down the line, taking half as much time to do both as I did to complete one.

Everyone applauded. Even Ashley's mom, Dr. Wong, had looked up from her reading to watch Frankie. He was something to see.

Coach Gilroy nodded his head and wrote

something down on his clipboard. It probably said something like, "That Townsend kid is great."

I wonder what he wrote about me on his clipboard. Probably something like, "That Zipzer kid is great at setting up cones."

Which, when I think about it, is pretty much my best soccer skill.

For the rest of the practice, Coach Gilroy gave us a long motivational speech about how we were no longer individuals but part of a winning team. And he must have pointed out at least six times that there is no "I" in "team."

As for me, I was trying to concentrate on what he was saying, but other things just kept rolling around in my mind.

CHAPTER 8

TEN THINGS THAT ROLL AROUND IN YOUR MIND WHEN YOUR COACH IS MAKING A MOTIVATIONAL SPEECH

1. I wonder what's for dinner. Whatever it is, I hope it involves French fries.
2. If French fries could talk, would they have a French accent?
3. If I had two tongues, would I still be able to whistle?
4. I wonder if red ants are really red, or are they just sunburned?
5. What would people look like if they had ankles where their knees are and knees where their ankles are?
6. What's the point of hair growing in your nose? Is it supposed to keep the inside of your nose warm?

7. Will they ever change the name of New York City to Old York City? I mean, it's not really so new anymore.

8. If pickles were blue, would I still like to eat them?

9. What if balls were square, would they still—*"Zipzer, did you hear anything I said?"*

"Oh yes, Coach Gilroy. Every word. And it is so interesting."

CHAPTER 9

WHEN YOU'VE HAD A BAD DAY at school, followed by a bad day at soccer tryouts, I think you should at least be able to come home and enjoy a great dinner. Say, a juicy burger, some crispy fries drenched in ketchup, maybe a big frothy chocolate milkshake. Finish with a dessert that leaves whipped cream all over your face— like banana cream pie or black cherry Jell-O. Yeah, that's a great bandage on a bad day.

In my house, there is no such thing as a hamburger and fries dinner. My mom runs the Crunchy Pickle deli, which when Papa Pete ran it served great food. But when my mom took it over, she promised to bring deli meats into what she calls "the realm of healthy eating." So in my house, we have healthy dinners that alternate between the realms of taste-free and taste-bad.

"Come to the table, everyone," my mom called that night. "Dinner's ready."

I leaped like a gazelle out of my desk chair, down the hall, across the living room, and into my dining room chair. My mom was just coming out of the kitchen carrying a platter that was steaming.

"Hope you don't mind being guinea pigs," she said. "It's a new recipe."

A new recipe? Oh, boy. She hasn't even gotten the old ones right yet.

Even though I tried to keep a straight face, my dad must have seen my nose twitch because he shot me one of his Stern Dad looks.

"Hank, your mother is being adventuresome," he said. "Replace that smirk with a smile."

Sure, that's easy for him to say. He wasn't counting on dinner to be the highlight of a very, very bad day. And besides, we all know that he keeps a stash of Baby Ruths in his nightstand to make up for adventuresome dinners.

"What have you cooked up, my darling daughter?" Papa Pete asked. My grandpa was there for dinner, which is a good thing because he's a very fun guy.

"Maybe it's better if we don't know," I said. My dad shot me another look.

"Hank, you have to learn to be supportive of other people's creativity," Emily said in her Miss Know It All voice, which by the way, is her only voice. My mom did look pretty excited to present her new dish, and I decided to put on my most positive attitude.

"Okay, Mom, tell us all about it," I said. "Spare no details."

"This is a festival of tofu," my mom said, gesturing to the plate that was filled with a beige, watery mess. "I've done three different preparations, including braised tofu with curried mango, shredded tofu with strained prunes, and steamed tofu in its natural juices."

Let me just say right now for the record, its natural juices smelled like McKelty's bad breath.

"So Emily, since you're so supportive of creativity, let's see you take the first helping." I gave her a big smile and passed the platter to her.

"Oh, I just remembered," she stammered. "I had a big snack at Robert's house before dinner, and wow, am I full."

"Maybe Katherine would like some," my mom said. "She always enjoys my cooking."

Katherine, the queen of the pet iguanas, usually sits on Emily's shoulder during our family dinners because my sister can't stand to be apart from reptiles for even a second.

My mom put a helping of the steamed tofu in its natural juices on Emily's plate. Katherine's long, grey tongue shot out of her mouth and snatched up a chunk of it. I thought she was going to swallow it, but suddenly, she flicked her tongue sideways and shot the tofu chunk against the window behind me. It stuck like it had suction cups.

I glanced over at Papa Pete and saw him biting his lower lip, the one that you can barely see because of his bushy mustache. He always does that when he wants to laugh but isn't supposed to.

"Emily, you know we don't tolerate throwing food at the table," my dad said. "Would you please remove the lizard and take her back to your room."

"She has a name, Dad, and you know it very well," Emily said.

"Yeah, Dad," I chimed in. "It's Big Kathy, the food slinger."

I could see Emily starting to get steaming mad. In fact, she looked like the steaming tofu, with smoke coming out of her ears.

"Everyone, settle down," my mom said. "No one has even tried the tofu yet. Give it a chance."

She dished up a big glob of it to all of us. Papa Pete took the first bite because he's brave and he's nice too. He tried the shredded tofu with strained prunes. He rolled it around in his mouth for a while, then took a big gulp of water to help it slide as quickly as possible down his throat.

"That is something my mouth has never experienced before," he said. "And it was quite an experience. Yes, it was."

The rest of the family dug in. I put a chunk of tofu on my fork, but I didn't have the guts to pop it in my mouth. Papa Pete caught my eye. "Just push it around on the plate," he whispered. "I brought your favorite snack for later."

I knew exactly what it was. A giant, crunchy dill pickle.

"So, Hank, tell us all how soccer tryouts went," my mom said as she chomped down on a big bite of her braised tofu with curried mango. There's nothing she loves better than having a family dinner with lots of conversation. I have never understood why sitting around a table talking is so much fun for adults, but I know it is.

Before I could answer, my dad chimed in.

"I'm so proud of you, Hank, for going out for the soccer team. It's a great sport. I don't know if I ever told you, but I played it myself as a boy. As a matter of fact, I might even have my shin guards in the storage room in the basement. Want to borrow them?"

I don't know which was worse. The bad-breath tofu on my plate, or the idea of my father's moldy old shin guards on my legs.

"Thanks a lot, Dad, but Coach Gilroy told us to get a special kind of shin guard so we can all have the same kind."

"Sounds like you're bonding with your coach," my dad said, "which is very good, because he'll give you a lot of playing time. Coaches are people, and they have their favorites."

"I might be his favorite, Dad, but my body is not," I said, trying to let him down easy.

"What are you talking about, Hank? You're fast. I can see you dribbling down that field and kicking those goals."

"Dad, all I can tell you is that my brain and my feet are not on the same field. My feet want to dribble, but my brain says no."

"You just have to concentrate, that's all. Focus."

There was that word again. Focus. Everyone tells me to focus all the time. That word makes me want to throw up. It's not like I don't try to focus. I try. I tell my brain to focus, and it runs the other way. Don't they know how bad it makes me feel that I can't do it?

Papa Pete cleared his throat and came to my defense. Thank goodness for Papa Pete.

"You know, Stan," he said, "some people are good at one game, other people are good at other games. I for one am good at bowling. Not so good at basketball. Maybe Hank should try his hand at some other games."

"Pete, that's the problem here," my dad said,

putting his fork down, which he does when he's having a Serious Talk. "Hank starts things and doesn't finish. If he started soccer and signed up for the team, he's made a commitment. He can't let the team down."

"Dad, exactly how am I helping the team by sitting on the bench, polishing it with my butt?"

"Don't you think you'll get to play, dear?" my mom asked.

"I'm the worst one on my team, Mom. And the coach let me know that loud and clear."

"But isn't playing soccer supposed to be about exercising and running around in the fresh air?" my mom said. "I think the point of playing a game is to play."

"If you're Frankie it is. If you're me, it's about setting up the cones. On a good day, I bet I'll get to carry the ball bag onto the field."

"Practice makes perfect, Hank," my father said, looking me square in the face. "You keep going to practice and trying your best, and the coach will notice you. Coaches reward effort."

I wanted to tell him that I sit in Ms. Adolf's

class for six hours a day and that's no fun. And then I go to soccer practice and get yelled at and that's no fun. I wanted to tell him that I wasn't having any fun, but my dad was already on to another topic, telling Emily how he was working the crossword puzzle with his left hand to exercise the other side of his brain.

So I didn't say anything. Then I heard something.

Plop.

The little chunk of tofu that Katherine had flung onto the window had slid down the window and landed with a plop on the floor. Cheerio, our wonderful pet dachshund, jumped into action, ran to the tofu, and lapped it up with glee. Then he let out a happy yip and started chasing his tail in a circle.

Maybe I should be a dachshund. They seem to have a lot of fun.

CHAPTER 1⓪

AFTER DINNER, I SAT on the floor of my room licking those little reinforcement circles and sticking them very, very carefully (did I mention carefully) over the three holes of every piece of loose-leaf paper we had bought for the new school year. While I was doing it, I noticed that my mind kept wandering to the Parade of Athletes. My brain wanted to think about that rather than think about gluing little circles onto little holes. That's understandable. After all, it was a much more interesting topic. My brain knew what it was doing.

I was thinking that maybe at the Parade of Athletes I'd demonstrate toe basketball, a game I made up where I flick my socks into the dirty clothes hamper with my toes. I wonder what Katie Sperling would think of that? Would she think that was cute? Or would she go for a real

athlete like Frankie? Toe basketball was definitely a risk.

I confess that, after a while, I got a little
bored putting the reinforcements on. I'm not
going to sit here and tell you I didn't put a
couple on my cheeks and nose and chin. They
looked like Native American war paint, only
the kind that comes from Staples. I even put
a couple on Cheerio's nose, which was cool
because his nose was so wet, I didn't have to
lick them. They just stuck on easily.

When my tongue got kind of dry, Cheerio
helped me out. I'd hold one of the circles in my
hand, Cheerio would give it a lick, and I'd put
it in place. It's not often that a dachshund can
really help get a guy organized for school, and
I'll bet Cheerio felt pretty good about it.

There was a knock on the door. I knew it
was Papa Pete because he has a special knock
that goes *dah-dah-dah–dum*. He says it's the
first four notes of Beethoven's Fifth Symphony,
which is his favorite symphony of all time. He
keeps telling me we have to listen to all of it
sometime so I can see what comes after those
first four notes.

"I just finished a rousing game of Yahtzee with Emily," Papa Pete said.

"Wow, how'd you get so lucky, Papa Pete?"

"One fine day, you're going to appreciate your sister."

"Today is probably not the day."

"Anyone I know here interested in a pickle snack?" Papa Pete asked.

"What do you say, Cheerio?" I asked him. "Feel like a pickle?"

Cheerio gave me a look. If dogs could talk, he would be saying, "I wouldn't eat a pickle if it were the last thing on earth. But if you happen to have a piece of steak . . ."

"Cheerio's not in the mood, but I'll join you," I said to Papa Pete.

We headed out to the balcony off our living room, and Papa Pete produced a brown paper bag with two pickles in it. Seriously, I think this was one of my favorite times of the week. Correction. Of the month. We pulled up two folding aluminum beach chairs we keep out there. They look completely out of place on a tenth-floor balcony in the middle of New York City. But Papa Pete and I, we don't care.

It was a warm night, what my mom calls Indian Summer. I don't think that has anything to do with Indians. I think it means that the warm days of summer last longer than they should. The sun was setting, and I craned my neck to peek around the apartment building next door. I could see a little slice of the Hudson River turning magenta in the sunset. Well, a little slice might be too big. It was a tiny sliver. But still, it was our view, and I loved it.

We could hear the traffic ten floors below moving up and down Broadway, people going home from work or out to dinner or just sitting in taxis waiting for the traffic to unsnarl. The cars looked like Matchbox cars from that high up, and the people walking up and down Broadway looked like Lego people. Not exactly like my favorite Lego guy who is the pirate with two swords in his hand, though. You walk up and down Broadway with two swords in your hands and you're going to have a long conversation with the New York City police.

"So what's it going to be?" Papa Pete asked, reaching into his brown bag. "The usual garlic dill—or if you're feeling adventuresome, why not try a sweet gherkin?"

"I'm up for an adventure," I said. "But, Papa Pete, if I don't like the gherkin, will you trade it for the garlic dill?"

"Of course I will. I never met a pickle I didn't like. The same goes for grandsons."

Papa Pete handed me a pickle and a napkin that I used to wrap the bottom end of it so it wouldn't squirt pickle juice all over my shorts. I took a bite.

"Trade," I said, sticking the sweet pickle out toward Papa Pete.

"I give you credit for trying something new," Papa Pete said, handing me his garlic dill. "You never know unless you try."

I took a bite of the garlic dill. Oh yeah, now that's what my mouth was looking for. It made my taste buds jump off my tongue and scream, "Hallelujah."

"So that was some conversation we had at dinner about soccer," Papa Pete said. "Doesn't sound like you're enjoying yourself."

"I'll keep at it, I guess," I said. "Dad wants me to stick with it."

"Sports are supposed to be fun," Papa Pete said.

"Not when your coach is hollering at you to do things you can't do."

"That certainly doesn't sound like much fun to me," Papa Pete said. "I just joined an indoor Ping-Pong club on Eighty-first and West End. Why don't you come with me sometime and give it a try?"

"Ping-Pong? That's a weird sport."

"What's weird about it? You hold the paddle. You hit the ball."

"It's a game old people play in the backyard. In socks and brown leather sandals."

"Not so fast, Hankie my boy. All kinds of people play. Old and young. Fat and thin. Short and tall. Wide and narrow. Black and white. Beige and red."

"I get it, Papa Pete."

"Good. Come with me tomorrow after school."

"I have soccer practice."

"Fine, I'll pick you up after practice and we'll walk over."

"What if I don't like it?"

"Then we'll trade. You'll give me back the Ping-Pong, and I'll give you back your soccer. Just like the pickle."

"No questions asked?"

"No questions asked."

Papa Pete took a bite of his pickle, and I took a bite of mine. All you could hear was the crunch, crunch, crunching of us eating our pickles. We were exactly in unison. It was a perfect moment. Until we heard a scratch, scratch, scratching of claws on the glass door that leads to the balcony. We turned around and saw Katherine the Ugly trying to get the door open.

"The lizard wants to join us," Papa Pete said.

He and I shot each other a look, then turned around and continued munching on our pickles. We were unison on that decision too.

Katherine stays inside, thank you very much.

CHAPTER 11

$$5677$$
$$\times \ 283$$
$$\overline{?????53}$$
$$?????0$$
$$\overline{???}$$

THE NEXT DAY, I got up in the morning, had some oatmeal with raisins and brown sugar, and went to school.

The main thing I have to say about the fifth grade is that it's just like fourth grade, only harder. The vocabulary words are longer. The math problems are longer. The recesses are shorter.

I'd tell you more about the fifth grade, but if it is so mind-numbing for me, I can just imagine what it would be for you.

So let's just say this chapter is finished.

CHAPTER 12

AFTER SCHOOL I WENT TO soccer practice. I tried kicking. I tried kicking and running at the same time. I tried dribbling the ball around the cones.

I fell down.

I got yelled at by Coach Gilroy.

I got up and I sat on the bench.

I continued to sit on the bench until my butt fell asleep and had dreams of actually being able to play. It never woke up.

Soccer practice was no fun at all.

So let's just say this chapter is finished too.

CHAPTER 13

YOU'D BETTER BELIEVE that after a day like that, I wasn't too thrilled about joining Papa Pete for a visit to his Ping-Pong club. Papa Pete, who always knows what I'm feeling without me having to say it, understood that I was not exactly enthusiastic, so he offered me a bribe to improve my mood.

"What'll it be, Hankie? A root-beer float at McKelty's Roll 'N Bowl, or a hot dog off Amir's cart?"

"How about both?"

"Both is not an option. You have to save room for one of your mother's delicious dinners."

Papa Pete laughed as we turned the corner onto Broadway. We headed up the block toward where Amir parks his hot-dog cart, dodging the crowds of people coming out of the subway. I was pretty sweaty—not from soccer practice, because bench warming does not work up perspiration, but from hurrying to keep up with Papa Pete. Even though he's sixty-nine years old, Papa Pete keeps up quite a pace. He always says, as long as you're walking, you've got to walk like you're going somewhere.

And we were going somewhere: to Amir's hot-dog cart, which was right past the subway station on 79th and Broadway. Amir waved to us as we came up. I was smiling already, just taking in the smells of those boiling frankfurters mixed with the brown mustard and relish. My mouth started to water like it was Niagara Falls.

"The usual," Papa Pete said to Amir. "One for me, and one for my grandson here."

Amir handed me my hot dog first. He knows that I like the regular dog with everything on it but the onions. I took my first bite real slowly, biting down and listening for the snap of the hot-dog skin that releases the wave of flavors into my mouth. *Snap!* There it goes. Hot-dog spices filled my mouth, then the brown mustard with a hint of relish. Man oh man, there is nothing like a snappy mustard-relish dog on the streets of New York City to help you forget a lousy day. I felt sorry for every kid who wasn't eating one. Wait a minute, that's not exactly true: I didn't feel sorry for Nick McKelty, because he's a big, obnoxious tick, but . . .

Wait a minute, Hank. How'd McKelty get in your mind? Get him out of there. He's ruining your hot dog. Oh, yeah . . . that's better.

I did feel bad for every other kid in the world, minus Nick McKelty, who wasn't enjoying that delicious sidewalk frankfurter.

Papa Pete ate his hot dog in three bites like he always does: front, middle, and end, wiping his big mustache for dribbles of mustard or bun crumbs.

"How's the old handlebars, Hankie?" he said. "Anything hanging off them?"

"You're all clear," I answered. Papa Pete made me promise a long time ago that if he ever had anything hanging off his handlebar mustache, I'd tell him right away. It's a big responsibility, but I love it that he trusts me to do it.

I walked and ate at the same time, and by the time I reached the last bite, we were at the corner of 81st and Broadway. We turned left as I stuffed the last piece of hot dog into my mouth. I like to leave a little bit of the frankfurter hanging out of the end of the bun so I can save the best bite for last.

"Here's the place," Papa Pete said, pointing to a stairway that led down into a subterranean storefront door.

"There's no sign," I noticed. Of course there wasn't. I mean, what's a sign above a Ping-Pong club going to say, the All-Night Ping-Pong Emporium? Who wants to be seen going into that?

I heard the room before I saw it. *Ping*, then *pong. Ping. Pong. Ping. Pong.* Multiply that times twelve, which was the number of Ping-Pong tables in the large, well-lit room, and you'll have the sound that filled my ears as we walked in.

At each table there were two people hitting the ball back and forth to each other. And when I say hitting, I mean smacking it. Ping-Pong balls were shooting across the nets like cannonballs.

Boy, was I surprised. I have to admit, I never knew the game was so fast.

And while I'm at it, let me admit another

thing: I expected all the people in there to be really old, like forty-eight or fifty-one. But when I looked around, I was stunned by who was playing there. At the first table, a huge man with dreadlocks flying all over the place was playing a woman in white shorts. Her hand moved so fast, you couldn't even see it holding on to the paddle.

"That's Wei Chang," Papa Pete whispered. "She played in the 1996 Olympics for China."

At another table, there was a large, hairy man with an accent that sounded like Count Dracula's playing another hairy man wearing a baseball cap. They were playing fast and furiously. And here's the amazing thing: The guy in the baseball cap was in a wheelchair. That's right, you heard me. He'd pop a wheelie in order to get to the corner of the table to get the ball. And when he hit the ball, it had a wicked spin.

There were all kinds of people playing, and a few others sitting in folding chairs watching. At the table on the very end, I noticed a tall Asian man playing a little kid. And when I say little, I mean, standing on a box little.

Wait a minute. I know that little kid.

It was Sam Chin, Mason's friend from kindergarten.

"Hey, Sam," I hollered. "It's me, Hank!"

"Shhhhh," Papa Pete whispered. "You never distract a player in the middle of a game."

Wow, these Ping-Pong people take their game very seriously.

"But I know him," I told Papa Pete. "He goes to my school."

"His father is the head teacher and owner of the club," Papa Pete said, pointing to the tall man rallying with Sam. "He's internationally ranked."

"Wow," I said. "He must be really good."

Before Papa Pete could answer, the tall man put his paddle on top of the Ping-Pong ball to keep it from rolling off the table and walked over to where we were standing. "Hello, Pete," he said. "And this is . . . ?"

"My grandson, Hank."

"Welcome to the club, Hank," he said. "My name is Winston Chin." He shook my hand. He had a big hand. Mine got lost in it.

"I see you're a soccer player," Mr. Chin said, looking at the cleats I had slung over my shoulder.

"Oh, yeah," I said. "I've been known to kick the ball a ways."

"We have many good athletes here," Mr. Chin said.

The people in there didn't exactly look like athletes. I mean, you didn't see a lot of big muscles or sweaty headbands or expensive tennis shoes. And certainly no big-muscled guys in ironed soccer shorts. They looked like regular people in street clothes, only with Ping-Pong paddles in their hands.

"I go to school with Sam," I said. "At PS 87."

"Come over and hit with him," Mr. Chin said. "You can use my paddle and I'll give you a few pointers."

"Oh, no," I said. "I'm not really into patio sports. I'm more of an outdoorsy, grassy sports kind of guy."

"We don't consider table tennis a patio sport here," Mr. Chin said. "It's highly competitive. It's a sport that requires the reflexes of the bobcat, the speed of the cheetah, and the craftiness of the fox."

"Wow, that's a lot of animals," I laughed.

"They should play this at the zoo."

I cracked myself up. I thought my joke was hysterical. When I stopped laughing, I noticed that Mr. Chin had never started. Even Papa Pete didn't crack a smile. Whoops, I guess I put my foot right in my mouth, tennis shoe and all.

"Okay," I said, feeling bad that perhaps I had insulted Mr. Chin and his club. "I'll give it a try."

I followed Mr. Chin to the table where Sam was still standing on his box waiting for me.

Great. I'm about to play a patio sport with a three-foot-tall kindergartner standing on a box, no less. The only good thing about this is that Nick McKelty isn't here to see me.

Thank goodness for small favors.

CHAPTER 14

TEN REASONS I AM GOING TO HATE PLAYING PING-PONG

1. I can't even see the ball as it whizzes by me.

2. I can hear it, but that's totally annoying—all that pinging and ponging gets on your nerves.

3. No one I know who is anyone I want to know ever even mentions Ping-Pong—except Papa Pete. But he talks about a lot of weird stuff, like whether green bell peppers taste the same as red bell peppers.

4. Every regular ball I know of is made of rubber. I can't figure out what Ping-Pong balls are even made of—besides air.

5. Everybody in the Ping-Pong club was at

least forty-eight, except for Sam, and he was five. I didn't see any other ten-year-olds there.

6. Everyone else I know plays dribbling sports. The only dribbling in Ping-Pong is the kind that comes from your mouth if you spill your 7UP.

7. You can't convince me that Ping-Pong is a real sport. I mean, when was the last time you saw an article about the World Series of Ping-Pong on the sports page?

8. My Uncle Gary likes to play Ping-Pong at the beach in his Speedos and orange rubber flip-flops. Enough said.

9. If Nick McKelty ever gets word that I'm a Ping-Pong player, he'll call me a pencil-neck, paddle-toting, weird-sport-playing geekoid. I'd rather not hear that for the rest of my life.

10. I don't think I really need to come up with a tenth reason, because I'm thinking 1–9 are quite enough to make my point.

CHAPTER 15

OKAY, YOU KNOW that list you just read? Ignore it. Forget you ever laid eyes on it. I'm sorry I wasted your time with it.

Why? Because Ping-Pong is fun! And not just regular, everyday kind of fun, either. It is fast and furious fun.

Mr. Chin showed me two different ways to hold the paddle. One is where you have to shake hands with it. Shaking hands with a piece of wood is a weird concept to wrap your mind around, but once you get that hello right, the paddle becomes your best friend.

The other way is called a pen hold. You have to slip the handle between your index and middle finger and hold it backward. Mr. Chin tried to show me that hold at least eight times, but I had to concentrate so hard on where my fingers were supposed to be that it never got comfortable. He didn't yell at me, though, or make me feel bad, like Coach Gilroy did.

"We'll go with the handshake hold," he just said, "if that's what makes you comfortable." And that was that.

I took the paddle and stood in back of the table.

"Back up, Hank. You're standing too close," Mr. Chin said.

"Sam's just a little guy," I whispered to him. "He's going to hit it real soft, so I want to be close."

"Don't be so sure," Mr. Chin said, and smiled. "Serve it up, Sammy."

Whoosh! In one swift move, Sam sent the ball careening over the net. I'm sure it hit my side of the table, because I heard it, but I swear to you, I never saw it go by. I felt so stupid just standing there holding my paddle. I never even got a chance to take a swing at the ball. My arm never left my side.

"Ping-Pong is a game of quick reflexes," Mr. Chin said.

Sam hit another ball to me, and this time I lunged for it. It just hit my paddle, went flying across the room, and bounced off the far wall.

I turned and looked at Papa Pete.

"Practice makes perfect, Hankie," was all he said.

"Are you right-handed?" Mr. Chin asked me.

"You're right," I said. "And I'm right. Right and right."

"Good, so you put your left foot slightly in front of your right foot, spread your feet shoulder width apart, and watch the ball as it comes to you. The most important thing is to concentrate on the ball."

Concentrate. There's that word again. Why is concentration so important? And why is it so hard for my brain to do?

I wonder if there's a brain garage somewhere where you can drive your brain in and they work on it while you wait. Replace the concentration gizmo. And while you're at it, give it an oil and lube job, too.

"Hank, are you listening to me?" It was Mr. Chin, who must have noticed that I was out there driving my brain around town.

"Yup," I said, pulling my brain out of the

garage and putting it back in my head where it belonged.

"When you hit the ball this time, follow through. Your paddle should wind up in front of your face so that you're looking at the blade, which is the part of the paddle you hit with."

Mr. Chin was a really good teacher, because when Sam served me the next ball, I hit it exactly where it was supposed to go. It made the perfect sound. I pinged!

Unfortunately, Sammy ponged, and when the ball came sailing back at me, I missed the next shot. I didn't care. I was really excited to have hit the ball correctly. It felt smooth as glass.

"You must always remember to practice the Three Cs, Hank," Mr. Chin said. "Concentration. Control. Confidence."

He made those three Cs sound so simple. If only they were.

I don't know where the next hour went, but wherever it went, it went someplace really fun. I played with Sam for another fifteen minutes, until his mom came to pick him up for dinner. Then the guy with the dreadlocks came over to my table.

"Hey, little mon. I'll rally with you," he said in an accent that sounded like he was singing.

"But you're really good," I said.

"This is how you get good, mon," he said. "Rally with everyone. That's what I did as a boy back in Jamaica."

Maurice—that was his name—played with me for another half hour. At first I was nervous, because I kept missing the ball and having to chase it all over the club. But he gave me lots of good pointers, and by the time we were finished, I could actually return the ball three or four times in a row.

"Hankie," Papa Pete said at last. "We have to go now. It's dinnertime."

"Just a few minutes more," I begged.

"Yeah, mon. Hank and I are in a groove," Maurice said.

"I don't want to make your mother mad at me," Papa Pete said. "We'll come back another time."

While I was looking for my backpack, Mr. Chin came up to me. "Here," he said, handing me a Ping-Pong paddle with red rubber on one side and black rubber on another side.

"You can borrow this paddle for a while. Keep it with you. Hold it. Let it become your friend."

"Wow—thanks, Mr. Chin."

"And here are two balls for you to practice with. Bounce them on the paddle and against a wall until you start to get the feel of it."

I couldn't believe everyone there was being so nice to me. Not like at the soccer field, when Coach Gilroy didn't even say good-bye to me that afternoon. Actually, he did kind of say good-bye, if you can call "Remember to bring your game face to next practice, Zipzer" a good-bye.

As we pushed open the door to climb the stairs back up to 81st Street, I was in the best mood.

"That was so cool," I said to Papa Pete. "Do you think if I practice really hard, I could beat Maurice?"

"It could happen," Papa Pete answered. "Although he is the Jamaican national Ping-Pong champion."

"He's the best player in all of Jamaica?"

"Last I checked, that's what champion means."

Wow. I, Hank Daniel Zipzer, just played the best of the best of the best. And he thought I was okay.

"Papa Pete, do you think I'm good enough to enter a tournament?"

"Not yet, Hankie. But there's always tomorrow."

As we walked down Broadway toward home, I was careful to hop over all the cracks in the sidewalk. I was making a wish, the same wish over and over, and I wanted it to come true.

I wished that I would win a Ping-Pong tournament and become the Ping-Pong Wizard of New York City. In my mind, I could already see the trophy. It was big. I mean, really big. It was so big that I could use it for a jungle gym if I wanted.

I couldn't wait to get home and start practicing.

CHAPTER 16

I MUST HAVE HIT THAT Ping-Pong ball against my bedroom wall twenty thousand times that night. Don't get me wrong. It's not like I became a Ping-Pong wizard or anything. I was able to get a second hit only about nine times, if that. But hey, that's nine more times than I ever did before.

I couldn't wait to tell Dr. Berger about this. She knows that I have difficulties with hand-eye coordination. When Dr. Berger first explained hand-eye coordination to me, I really didn't pay that much attention. What she was talking about seemed really complicated. But when I started to practice hitting the Ping-Pong ball against the wall, it became crystal clear that this hand-eye coordination thing was a problem for me.

"There's the ball," my brain said as the ball bounced off the wall.

"Where?" my eyes said.

"Right there."

"Whoops, we missed it," my eyes answered.

My other problem was that it was really hard to keep track of the ball. I'd start seeing it, and then it would magically disappear. The next thing I knew, I'd hear it hit the leg of my desk and roll under my bed with the dust bunnies.

"Just keep watching the ball, Hank," I said to myself. "How hard is that?"

Apparently, really hard for my particular brain.

I remember when I was in kindergarten and went to David Platt's birthday party. The party favor was one of those wooden paddles with the rubber ball on a rubber band. Everyone else grabbed their paddle from the party-favor bag and started hitting the ball. They smashed that ball up and down, back and forth on the paddle. Not me. When I tried, my ball went in every direction—hit me in forehead, even. I could never get it, so I made up an excuse and told everyone that I wasn't in the mood to play with paddles and I was going to do it at home. When I got home, I put that paddle in the party bag, where it stayed pretty much forever. I can admit it to you now: I hate that toy.

As I practiced hitting the Ping-Pong ball, though, I was determined to get it right. I just planted my feet in my room, sunk my toes into my carpet, and hit that little white ball against the wall over and over and over.

"Hank," Emily shouted from her room. "That sound is driving Katherine nuts."

"She's already nuts. How would you know the difference?"

"Kathy and I do not appreciate your sarcasm. And, just for your information, she's trying to hide behind the twig in her cage and her eyes are blinking up a storm."

"Maybe her eyelids are sending you a message in Morse code: 'You are weird, and everyone knows it.' "

"Iguanas blink when they're stressed!" Emily shouted. "If you knew even the slightest bit about reptiles, you'd know that."

"Here's a news flash for you. My brain rejects all reptile knowledge."

Our voices must have gotten very loud, because my dad appeared at my bedroom door. I could tell he had been working on a crossword puzzle because he was wearing two pairs of glasses, one on his forehead and one on his eyes, and his blue mechanical pencil was shoved behind his ear.

"Hey, hey, what's going on in here?"

"Hank keeps hitting that stupid ball against the wall," Emily said, coming to the door of my room. "It's driving Katherine and me crazy."

"Don't annoy your sister," my dad said. "Enough for tonight."

"But, Dad, you always tell me that practice makes perfect. How am I going to get great at my new sport if I don't practice?"

"Ping-Pong is not a sport. It's a hobby."

"Not true."

"Yes, true. Soccer is your sport. Ping-Pong is your hobby. And doing well in the fifth grade is your goal. Now, don't you have homework to finish?"

Why is everything always about homework with him? It's like there's only one subject rattling around in his head. Did you do your *homework*? How much *homework* do you have? How's your *homework* coming? Did you finish your *homework*? You can't listen to music when you're doing your *homework*. Why don't you start on tomorrow's *homework*? It's good to get a leg up on your *homework*.

"I just have a math worksheet," I said. "I'll get up early and finish it."

"No, you won't, because I happen to know you have a dentist appointment tomorrow morning," Emily the walking calendar reported.

She was right. Somewhere way back in my brain, I remember my mom saying that I had a tooth-cleaning appointment with Dr. Crumbworthy. That man talks about flossing like regular people talk about baseball or movies or comic books. He just lights up at the mention of it. And you should see him demonstrate the correct flossing method. He actually breaks out in a sweat from it.

So here's what I was looking at. Do math homework. Go to bed. Get up extra early. Go to dentist. Listen to him scrape my teeth with that pointy metal thing of his.

I looked at the Ping-Pong paddle in my hand. Just a minute ago, we were having a really good time.

Boy, how a night can change.

CHAPTER 17

DR. CRUMBWORTHY IS MISSING the fourth finger on his left hand. Well, actually not the whole finger, just the part that has the fingernail on it. Ordinarily, that wouldn't be such a big deal, but when a guy has his hands in your mouth and he's missing part of a finger, you wonder if another fingertip is going to fall off on your tongue. At least, that's what I was wondering while he poked around in my mouth with his mirror and silver pointy thing.

"How's life treating you, Hank?" he said.

"Ine," I answered. Okay, you try to say *fine* when you have a mouth of metal and fingers going into all different parts of your mouth.

"Doing well in school?" he asked.

Why is that always the second question adults have to ask you after finding out about your health? I mean, why can't they ask if you've seen any funny movies or had a great slice of pizza or ridden on a really cool roller-coaster? You'd think a guy like Dr. Crumbworthy would know better. He's a kids' dentist, and everyone in my neighborhood goes to him to have their teeth cleaned and their cavities filled. He should have learned by now that kids don't really want to discuss how they're doing in school when that instrument with that little hook at the end is in your molars looking for cavities.

"Ure," I answered. *S*'s are hard too.

"Is there any reason you have a Ping-Pong paddle in your lap?" he asked.

I forgot to mention that I was holding the Ping-Pong paddle while I was at the dentist's. I had two reasons. First, because Winston Chin had told me to carry it around everywhere and make it my friend, and I took that very seriously. And second, because I thought that in case Dr. Crumbworthy poked me too hard, I could hold up the red side of the paddle and wave it around like a stop sign.

There was no way I could explain all of that to Dr. Crumbworthy with his nine and a half fingers in my mouth. It wasn't really necessary, anyway, because he likes to keep the conversation going all by himself. I guess you learn to do that when the people you're talking to can't answer.

"There is nothing like a good game of Ping-Pong at the end of the day," he said. "Have you discovered the Ping-Pong Emporium over on 81st?"

I nodded. How did he know about our club?

"That's a great place," he said. "I've been playing there for a couple years."

Wow, it was lucky I hadn't run into him the day before.

"It gets pretty hot in there by the end of the night. I like to wear a tank top and sweats, but when I get really sweaty, I peel off my sweats and rally in my Speedos."

At that thought, I almost bit his finger off. I'm not kidding. Dr. Crumbworthy doesn't know how close he came to having eight and a half fingers.

"You should try it," he said. "Just wear Speedos under your sweats."

I didn't have the heart to tell him, and he

wouldn't have been able to understand me, anyway, but I'll play Ping-Pong in my Speedos on the day the Mississippi River flows backward.

"I've got a great backhand," he went on. "Even Maurice can't get anything by me when I unleash my wicked topspin."

This was so weird. Two days ago I would have thought this conversation was crazy, and now I'm understanding everything he's saying.

Wow, Hank Zipzer, when did you become a Ping-Pong know-it-all?

"I'm thrilled to see you taking up the sport," Dr. Crumbworthy went on. "Not a lot of young people your age understand the excitement that Ping-Pong has to offer."

Suddenly, Dr. Crumbworthy took his hands out of my mouth and spun around.

"I've got a great idea!" he said. He went to a keyboard he keeps on a shelf in his office and started to type.

One thing I haven't told you about Dr. Crumbworthy's office is that there's an electronic banner running along his wall that flashes the news of kids in his practice. It's like the runner you see at the bottom of a TV screen if you watch a news channel, which I never personally do. But instead of flashing news about the president's trip to Europe, or the baseball scores, his flashes contain news like "Congratulations to Heather Payne for trying minty dental floss." Or, "Hats off to Luke Whitman for using a toothbrush instead of his fingers." My sister Emily's name is always flashing up there for getting the "Clean Teeth Award." Not only for her but for Katherine, which isn't that easy since iguanas have 188 teeth to keep clean.

As Dr. Crumbworthy typed, I watched the red letters flash up on the screen. I recognized my name, of course, as it rolled by. But since I'm not the fastest reader in the world, the message had to scroll by a couple of times before I could read the whole thing. It said, "Congratulations to Hank Zipzer for exploring the excitement of Ping-Pong!"

I have to admit, it felt pretty good to see my name up in lights, flashing like one of the Mets' names on the big scoreboard at Shea Stadium.

Even when Dr. Crumbworthy started poking around in my mouth again, I didn't mind. My brain was busy. I was thinking that if I won some tournaments, I could get Dr. Cumbworthy to post my scores. Everyone in my school would see, even Kim Paulson. She'd think they were cute. I'd get famous and people would ask for my autograph on the street. I'd go to the Olympics on the American Ping-Pong team. My picture would be on a box of cereal, with a tiny Hank Zipzer doll inside, wrapped in cellophane.

"Oooowww." The sound came flying out of my mouth before I could stop it. I held the red side of the paddle up in the air.

"I'm sorry, Hank, did I nick your gums?" Dr. Crumbworthy asked.

"It's okay," I told him, "because I want my teeth to look really good when they take my picture for the cereal box."

Dr. Crumbworthy looked confused. He didn't know what I was talking about, but he'd find out soon enough.

CHAPTER 18

AT MY SCHOOL, when you come in late from a dentist appointment, the first thing you have to do is check in with Mrs. Crock at the attendance office, which is just outside Principal Love's office.

Mrs. Crock is a really nice person, but she takes a long time to fill out a late pass. She types one word on her computer, then takes a bite of the salad that is always sitting in a little plastic bowl next to her.

"Hi, Hank. I assume you have a note from your dentist," she said, smiling at me and showing a bit of radish between her teeth. Or maybe it was tomato. Whatever it was, it definitely had come from her salad bowl.

"Here it is," I said, pulling the note out of my back pocket along with some light blue lint and a green Tic Tac.

While I waited for her to finish the pass, I noticed a big piece of poster board on the wall. It was the sign-up sheet for the Parade of Athletes. A whole bunch of kids had already signed up. Joelle Adwin had signed up to do a gymnastics demonstration. A third-grader named Christopher Hook had signed up for trampoline. Frankie and Ashley were going to demonstrate soccer dribbling and passing. Funny, they hadn't asked me. Sarah Stern, a really sweet girl in Emily's class, was doing karate. Sam Chin had signed up for Ping-Pong. And Nick McKelty had the unbelievable nerve to sign up for advanced soccer drills. The only thing he was advanced at was tripping over his own big feet.

Finally, Mrs. Crock finished, but just as I was leaving the office, Principal Love appeared. He has this mole on his cheek that is shaped like the Statue of Liberty—and both he and the Statue of Liberty mole were giving me a nasty look. I'm not kidding, I think the mole was frowning at me.

"Late again, I see," Principal Love said.

"Oh no, sir, not late. I was at the dentist's."

I tried to slide out the door so I could get to recess. Principal Love is not known for his short conversations.

"Ah, oral hygiene. One of my favorite topics."

Please don't say any more, Principal Love. I'm begging you.

"Like I always say, good oral hygiene is what makes a man a man and a tooth a tooth," he said. I could tell he was gearing up to repeat himself, like he always does.

This time he surprised me, though. He didn't repeat himself.

"Is that a Ping-Pong paddle you're holding?" he asked.

Before I even got a chance to say yes, he cleared his throat and went on.

"I don't mean to brag, but I am proud of the fact that I earned a merit badge in table tennis at Boy Scout Camp in Minnesota."

My foot was tapping. It felt like there was a train engine in it.

"Sir, I am really fascinated by your summer in Minnesota, and I can't wait to hear more about it. But it's just that, right now, I've got to—"

"Of course you've got to get to class. Education comes first at PS 87. Like I always say, education comes first at PS 87." Bingo, there it was. The repeat!

As I slipped out of the office and scooted down the hall, I could hear him talking to Mrs. Crock.

"Have I ever told you about my superior skill with a Ping-Pong paddle?" I heard him ask.

"Many times, Principal Love," I heard her say with a sigh.

I ran out the double doors into the September sun that was heating up the school yard, looking around for Frankie and Ashley. They were waiting in line for a turn on the handball court.

"Hey, Zip," Frankie said. "How'd it go with Dr. C? Did he do that close breathing thing again?"

"Yeah, but this time I tried to hold my breath as long as I could. Listen, Frankie, did you know that Dr. Crumbworthy is a Ping-Pong player?"

I'll be honest. I was fishing around to see what his reaction would be when I mentioned the game. Obviously, he didn't think much of it.

"No kidding, dude. Did you know that my aunt Eleanor is a five-time shuffleboard champion? Maybe we should fix them up."

Frankie, one. Ping-Pong, zero.

"I'm serious, Frankie. He plays with the Ping-Pong champion of Jamaica."

"No way!" Frankie laughed. "Jamaica has a Ping-Pong champion?"

Frankie, two. Ping-Pong, still zero.

"Nerd alert! Did somebody just say Ping-Pong? I wouldn't play that game if you paid me."

It was McKelty, who had just finished his turn at handball.

"Where did you come from, and who asked your opinion, anyway?" Ashley said. She loves to speak her mind to McKelty.

"No one has to ask me," McKelty said. "It's my opinion that Ping-Pong is for subhumans."

"Then you're probably great at it," Ashley said. Frankie cracked up.

Ashweena, one. McKelty, zero.

"Is that supposed to be funny?" McKelty said. That's the thing about McKelty. He gets jokes about a year after they're said.

"Ping-Pong doesn't get much respect here," Ashley said, "but my relatives back in China are really good at it."

"This is New York City, not China," McKelty said. "China is all the way just past England."

"McKelty, don't you know anything?" Ashley said.

"I know one thing. The only people I've ever heard of who play Ping-Pong are senior citizens. And I don't mean just grandparent-old. I mean old-old."

I decided then and there that McKelty would never find out that I played Ping-Pong. Thank goodness I had stashed my paddle in my backpack before I'd come out on the yard.

"In fact, did you know that Dr. Crumbworthy is a Ping-Pong nut? But when you have nine fingers, that's all you can play," McKelty continued.

"I don't think it's nice to make fun of someone because he has a disability," Ashley said. "I think it's cool that he's learned to handle all those sharp instruments when he's missing a fingertip."

"Don't remind me. I have to see him this

afternoon after school," McKelty said. "Got to keep the old choppers in shape."

How a guy can think that his choppers are in shape when they point in every direction on a compass is amazing to me.

"Hey, Hank," a little voice called from behind us. We all turned around to see Sam Chin, all three feet of him, running toward me holding his Ping-Pong paddle.

I tried to pretend I didn't see him. I certainly didn't want to tell McKelty that I was into Ping-Pong, and Frankie's cool reaction to the topic was holding me back from telling him and Ashley, too. That was crazy, though. Everyone knows you can't ignore a kindergartner who's trying to get your attention.

"You want to practice playing Ping-Pong with me against the wall?"

McKelty grinned at me, showing his snaggly tan teeth.

"You play Ping-Pong, Zip Butt?"

"No way," I said. "I don't know what you're talking about."

"Sure you do, Hank," Sam chimed in. "Remember last night!"

"What's the little dude talking about?" Frankie asked, giving me a funny look.

"Hey, Sam, I just happen to have a fresh, chocolate Ding Dong that I traded a granola bar for," I said. "It's got your name written all over it."

"It does?"

"Yeah, come with me. I'll show you."

I grabbed Sam's hand and nearly pulled him right out of his shirt. I couldn't get him away from that group fast enough. My heart was pounding. The last thing I wanted was for McKelty to discover my secret life as a Ping-Pong wizard. I'd hear about that for the rest of my life, and then some.

"You've gotta promise me, Sam, to never say that we play Ping-Pong together," I whispered to him as I handed over the Ding Dong.

"Why? Didn't you have fun?"

"That's not the point."

"Then what is?"

"You don't like it when people make fun of you, right? And neither do I. Some kids are going to tease me if they find out I play Ping-Pong."

"That's silly."

"Well, that's the way life is in the fifth grade."

"Then I think I'll stay in kindergarten. Want to stay in kindergarten with me and Mason?"

"Sometimes I wish I could, little guy. I really do."

CHAPTER 19

ABOUT TWENTY MINUTES LATER, I was sitting in class copying my vocabulary words from the board to my notebook when it hit me like a bolt of lightning.

"Oh, no!" came flying out loud and clear before I got control of my brain and my mouth.

Ms. Adolf looked at me and headed down my aisle. "What's the problem, Henry?"

The problem was that I had just realized that Nick McKelty was going to be sitting in the dentist's chair that afternoon. And what was going to flash in front of his eyes, in red letters, over and over again?

"Congratulations to Hank Zipzer for exploring the excitement of Ping-Pong."

He would read that, and then my life as I knew it would be over.

I had to erase those red letters before he saw them. But how?

The answer was Joelle Adwin.

"Psst, Joelle," I whispered to her after Ms. Adolf had gone back to the board. Joelle didn't look up. I tore off the bottom of the paper that had my vocab words on it and scratched out a note.

"Need to borrow your sell fone. Ugent," I wrote.

I folded the paper into a tiny wad and passed it to Luke Whitman, who had to pull two of his fingers out of his mouth before he could take the note. I'm sure the note was soggy from his spit when he passed it to Heather Payne. She looked at me and shook her head no, like she wasn't going to pass it to Joelle. I shot her my best desperate look, the one where my mouth droops down and my eyes get half closed. That worked, because she passed the soggy wad to Joelle.

Joelle was just starting to open it up when Ms. Adolf turned from the board and made a beeline for her desk.

"Joelle, perhaps you'd like to share this note with the entire class," Ms. Adolf said.

"I don't even know what it says," Joelle said. "It's kind of stuck together."

"Allow me to assist you," Ms. Adolf said, and very carefully peeled the note open with her grey fingernails. "And who is the author of this damp communication?" she asked.

Three fingers all pointed in my direction: Joelle's, Heather's, and Luke's. Luke's finger had a small wad of already-been-chewed Milky Way that he had finally managed to pry out of his back tooth.

"Henry, the same rule applies in the fifth grade as it did in the fourth grade," Ms. Adolf snapped. "And that rule would be what?"

"I know that, Ms. Adolf. That rule would be to always use lined notebook paper, and not the kind with the skinny little lines."

A few people in the class started to laugh. I wasn't trying to be funny, though, because one time I accidentally bought a whole pack of the skinny-lined paper and I almost went blind trying to write letters small enough to fit into them.

"The rule that was in my mind, Henry, was that we do not pass notes in class."

"Oh, I was going to say that one next."

She looked down at the note and read it over, then gave me what you'd have to call a pretty harsh look that shot right through her glasses. I'm surprised the lenses didn't crack. If this was a cartoon, they would have. But my life is all too real, because the next sentence out of her mouth was—

"And for your information, young man, urgent has an *r*, cell as in cell phone is spelled with a *c*, and phone starts with a *ph* and not an *f*."

"I've made a mental note of that, Ms. Adolf."

The entire class was splitting a gut, and if she wasn't riled up enough before, let me just say that that did it.

"Why don't you take your note to Principal Love's office so he can see how you're spending precious class time."

Oh no, she's sending me to the principal's office and it's only the fourth day of the fifth grade.

Wait a minute, Hank! Principal Love's office is just inside the attendance office. And what's in the attendance office, you ask?

A phone.

That's right. Sitting smack in the middle of Mrs. Crock's desk.

I ran all the way down three flights of stairs, through the long hall, and burst into the attendance office, skidding to a stop right in front of Mrs. Crock's desk.

"I'll tell you in a minute why I'm here," I panted, "but before that, can I use your phone right away? It's an emergency."

Mrs. Crock pushed the phone over to me, and I picked up the receiver. It was at that moment that I realized I had no idea what Dr. Crumbworthy's phone number was.

"May I call information?" I asked Mrs. Crock.

"Hank, this phone is for emergencies only, not for social calls."

"But this is important."

"I'm sorry, Hank. If it were up to me, I'd let you, but this is a firm school rule."

Just then, Principal Love walked out of his office and spotted me.

"Well, Mr. Zipzer, I see you've been sent to my office already," he said. "Starting the school year off on the wrong foot will definitely involve your other foot as well. So I suggest you walk them right into my office and take a seat. I believe you're well acquainted with the chair."

I've spent so much time in that chair, I swear the shape of my butt is imprinted on it.

"Principal Love, am I right in guessing that if I asked you if I could make a phone call first, you'd probably say no?"

"How right you are," he said.

The rest of the day remained completely phoneless. It wasn't until Papa Pete came to pick me up after school that I was able to get in contact with Dr. Crumbworthy. Papa Pete let me use his cell phone. He's the kind of guy who knows that when you say you have to make an important call, you just have to do it, no questions asked.

"Dr. Crumbworthy," I said, after his assistant, Paula, put me on hold and had me listen to a country-western song for the looongest two minutes of my life.

"What's so important, Hank?" he asked.

"You've got to erase that Ping-Pong item about me from your news flashy thingamajig."

"Why? You were so proud of it just a few hours ago."

"Because Nick McKelty thinks Ping-Pong is for subhumans and he's called me enough names in my life and I don't need him to call me subhuman, too."

"Nick McKelty? He's sitting with his father in my waiting room right now."

"Please, Dr. Crumbworthy, I beg you. Hang up right now and erase it. I'll floss my teeth five times a day, I promise."

"Now that's what I call a deal," Dr. Crumbworthy said. "Don't you worry, Hank. I'll take care of it right away."

"Thanks a million trillion," I said.

Phew, that was close. As I clicked off the phone and handed it back to Papa Pete, he gave me a curious look. "What was that all about?" he asked.

Boy, that was a big question.

CHAPTER 20

W<small>E LEFT THE SCHOOL</small> and walked down 78th Street toward Broadway. Papa Pete was quiet, which means he was waiting for my answer.

"I could really go for a slice of pizza," I said, trying to fill the silence.

"Let's go to Harvey's. Afterward, I thought you might want to go hit some balls at the Ping-Pong Emporium."

"I think I'll get the white pizza with spinach and garlic," I said, trying to avoid the Ping-Pong topic.

We stopped into Harvey's, which was right on our way. I got a slice of the white pizza with a 7UP, and Papa Pete got pepperoni with a root beer. We walked the three blocks up to 81st Street in silence, just enjoying our pizza and sipping our drinks.

Papa Pete waited until I had finished my slice before he spoke again. "I'm waiting," he said.

"I know you are, Papa Pete," I answered. "This Ping-Pong thing has gotten pretty complicated all of a sudden. Nick McKelty thinks only old people and subhuman nerds play Ping-Pong."

"Which is why you wanted your dentist to keep it a secret."

Boy, Papa Pete is good at figuring things out. He'd put the whole thing together just like that.

"I get teased enough," I said. "I don't need more."

"No one needs to be teased," Papa Pete said. "But you can't keep what you do a secret. Especially if you enjoy it."

"Yeah, and there's something else, too," I said. "I feel kind of bad saying this."

"Better out than in," Papa Pete said. "Let it rip."

"I haven't even told Frankie or Ashley that I'm playing Ping-Pong," I said. "I was going to, but now I don't want to."

"Because you're ashamed?"

"Well, I kind of hinted around to Frankie

that I was thinking of taking it up."

"And?"

"And he compared it to his aunt Eleanor playing shuffleboard."

"Frankie's your friend, Hankie. He'll learn to respect what you choose to do."

"There's something else. I keep thinking that if I tell Ashley and Frankie, then they'll want to play, too."

"And that wouldn't be fun?"

"It's just that they're both such good athletes. They'd pick up a paddle and be great and leave me in the dust. I'd like something that I'm good at all by myself."

Papa Pete nodded but didn't say anything.

"Does it make me a terrible person for thinking these things?"

"No, it just makes you a person."

"So would it be all right to keep my secret Ping-Pong life a secret for a while?"

"That's up to you, Hankie. My lips are sealed."

By then, we had reached the Ping-Pong Emporium. Papa Pete held the door open for me. As I went inside, I was hit by a chorus of

"Hi, Hank." There they all were: Winston Chin, Sammy Chin, Maurice, and Niko, the guy in the wheelchair. They'd all remembered my name.

And not only that, they were asking if I wanted to play. They weren't telling me to take a knee and put on my game face and sit on the bench or wait my turn or set up the cones. They were just asking me to play.

I waved to them all, got out my paddle, and joined a rally going on at one of the tables.

Wow, suddenly I knew why everybody loves to play sports.

It's fun.

CHAPTER 21

FOR THE NEXT WEEK AND A HALF, Papa Pete picked me up every day after school and we raced directly to the Ping-Pong Emporium. Okay, the truth is, we didn't race directly there, we stopped first at Harvey's to get a slice of pizza. But understand, this wasn't just your regular social slice of pizza. We were fueling up for a workout. When you play Ping-Pong, you need energy and focus and reflexes. It just so happens that pizza gives you all those things. And it tastes great, too.

As each day passed, I got better and better. I didn't notice it at first. I was just trying to hit the ball back and forth and feel like one of the guys. I played with Papa Pete and Sammy Chin. They were both so patient when I kept hitting the ball off the table. Everyone taught me something different. Mr. Chin, who said I could call him Winston, showed me footwork so I didn't keep getting my feet tangled up in a knot. And we worked on the Three Cs—concentration, control, and confidence. Maurice showed me how to hold the ball when you serve so your opponent can't see it coming. Niko taught me how to watch the ball so you can predict where it's going before it even gets there. He had to learn that early on since he plays from a wheelchair.

One day, and I can't tell you if it was the seventh or eighth day after I'd started playing, I suddenly realized that I was getting the rhythm of the game. I could just feel it. Ping-Pong is all about rhythm.

Ping. Winston Chin hits the ball to me. *Pong.* It whizzes by my ear.

Ping. He hits it again. *Pong.* I go for it, but all I see is air.

Ping. Another ball whizzing toward me.

Pong. I get a paddle on it but hit it into the net.

Ping. Fast serve coming down my throat. I duck.

Pong. I stick my paddle out and pray. The

ball hits my paddle, clears the net, but goes long and bounces off the table next to us.

Ping. Another serve, spinning toward me in mid-air.

Pong. Oh yeah, I return it, smack down the middle.

Ping. Sammy smashes a looping ball at me.

Pong. My paddle and hand are in the right place at the right time. I hit a solid return. A thrill goes through me.

I had to learn different shots, and trust me, they're more complicated than they look. There's sidespin, topspin, backspin, the slam, the kill, the push, the loop. Papa Pete is the master of the topspin. When he hits it, the ball looks like it's going in five different directions. When I try to return them, they keep ricocheting off the edge of my paddle.

I've got to figure this out. Concentration. Control. Confidence. Here it comes. You can hit! No you can't—you just hit it into the net.

I don't always keep trying at things that are hard for me. Sometimes I give up. But I was loving Ping-Pong and I was determined to keep going until I got it.

Ping. Papa Pete serves it up.

Pong. I get my paddle up to block the ball. Miss.

Ping. Another curveball coming straight at me.

Pong. Got my paddle on it. Not a great shot, but it goes over the net.

Ping. Here comes a killer serve. I didn't even see it coming.

Pong! I lunge for it. Got it! Unbelievable! I return that serve.

I'm sweating, moving my feet like lightning. I bounce from foot to foot, shifting my weight so that no matter what direction the ball takes, I'll be there.

For weeks, I played full-out, heads-up, total-body Ping-Pong for two hours every day. It really took a lot of concentration. I never knew I had so much concentration. It's amazing what your brain can do when you put your mind to it.

Look at you, Hank. Weeks ago you didn't even know how to hold your paddle. And now you're holding your own.

It was for real, too. I'm sure the guys at the

club weren't giving me a break. I was becoming a player. One of them.

I didn't mind that I had to practice all the time. As a matter of fact, I looked forward to it. It was making me feel great.

Ping. Pong. Ping. Pong. Ping. Pong. Ping. Pong.

Look at me, world. I'm pinging and ponging!

CHAPTER 22

"WHERE HAVE YOU BEEN, MAN? It's like you've disappeared," Frankie said when he called me on the phone before dinner Thursday night.

"Here and there."

"Don't 'here and there' me, man. Something's up. You've been missing soccer practice. You didn't sign up for the Parade of Athletes. You're not at home when I call. What's going on?"

"I can't tell you," I said.

"You can't tell me? When was the last time there was anything we couldn't tell each other?"

"I want to tell you, Frankie, but I can't right now. I . . . I . . . I . . . have to go talk to my dad."

"Zip, be in the clubhouse after dinner. We're having a meeting."

It wasn't entirely a lie that I had to go talk to my dad. He had dropped a bomb that Coach Gilroy had called to "discuss" my attendance at practice, and now my dad wanted to "discuss" the phone call with me. When grown-ups say they want to discuss something, it never means that they want to discuss something fun, like the Mets' batting order or what flavor birthday cake you want. In my house, *discuss* means trouble is right behind.

"Sit down, Hank, I want to have a discussion," my dad said after I hung up the phone and went into the living room. "The coach called to see if you're feeling better. He thought you were sick."

"I'm not sick."

"Apparently you haven't been attending practice on a regular basis."

"Yeah, Dad, I've been meaning to discuss that with you."

"I'm right here, Hank. Discuss away."

"Well, the greatest thing has happened, Dad. I've found a new sport, and I think I'm going to be good at it."

"Wait, now you're going to play two sports?"

"Not exactly, Dad. You know how you always say that if you want to be really good at something, you have to concentrate on it? See, I've taken those words very seriously. Very, very seriously."

"And exactly what is this 'it' you're concentrating on?"

"Ping-Pong." I must have said it softly, which I do when I'm not sure I want to be saying something at all. In fact, I said the words so softly, I'm not sure I could even hear them myself.

"I don't think I heard you correctly," my dad said.

I cleared my throat, clenched my fist, and shouted out the truth.

"Ping-Pong. I've been playing Ping-Pong at Papa Pete's club, and Dad, I really think I'm getting good at it."

"And did it ever occur to you that you have a responsibility to Coach Gilroy and your soccer team? That you're letting them down?"

"Not exactly, Dad. The bench is doing just fine without my butt on it."

"I'm disappointed in you, Hank."

There it was. The awful *D* word. But why? Why would he be disappointed? I didn't have to wait long to find out.

"My disappointment has several facets to it," my dad began.

Oh boy, he isn't just regular disappointed. He's several-faceted disappointed. This isn't looking good.

"First of all, you have essentially quit the soccer team without discussing it with your family."

Why can't I pick my own sport without discussing it with the whole family? I mean, Katherine is a member of our family. Is that beady-eyed reptile supposed to tell me how to spend my sporting time?

"Second," my dad went on, "you have been irresponsible to Coach Gilroy and your teammates in not letting them know your plans."

Irresponsible? Coach Gilroy is so glad not to have me anywhere near his field, he's probably jumped up and down so much that his cleats got stuck in the grass. I'll bet the only way he can get off the field is to untie his shoes and leave them there.

"Third, while Ping-Pong is a nice backyard pastime, I certainly don't consider it a sport. It doesn't command the respect of the athletic community."

It commands my respect. Isn't that what matters?

"So, Hank, what do you have to say for yourself?" my dad asked.

"I just thought I was having a wonderful time doing something fun," I said. "I didn't know it would make you so upset."

"Well, now you know. That's what discussions are for."

There was a long silence. It was obvious that my dad was waiting for me to say something.

"I'm waiting," he said. As if I hadn't noticed.

"I guess you want me to give soccer another try." I was talking really softly again.

"The thought has occurred to me. And I know that decision will make you feel good about yourself."

Which self is that? Whatever self it is, I've certainly never met it.

"Your sister mentioned that tomorrow night

is the Parade of Athletes at school," my dad said. "I understand some of your friends are preparing to demonstrate their soccer skills. That sounds like fun."

Fun? Getting up in front of the whole school and making a fool of myself? Wow, that does sound like fun.

"I'd like you to join in, Hank."

What I was thinking was—*he's my father, and I'm his son. How can our feelings about the same subject be so far apart?*

But what I said was, "I can't, Dad. I already missed the sign-ups."

"That's too bad," he said.

I don't think so. I couldn't have been more relieved.

CHAPTER 23

I WAS QUIET ALL THROUGH DINNER. Emily was chattering about how she got 100 percent on both her spelling test and her geography quiz.

"Hank, why aren't you participating in the family conversation?" my mom asked, noticing my silence.

"Fine," I said, and turned to Emily. "Don't you ever get anything but one hundred percents?"

"Sure, I do," Emily answered. "I got one hundred and ten percent on my math test. Extra credit for the bonus problem."

That was a conversation ender if ever I heard one. I shoved another bite of my tofurkey taco in my mouth.

After dinner, I went down to the clubhouse to meet Frankie and Ashley. Our clubhouse is in a storage room in the basement, and it's a place where we can talk and be alone.

When I walked in, Frankie and Ashley were sitting on the old couch we keep there. Before I could say a word, they both pointed to something behind the door.

"Beware! We are not alone," Ashley said.

I peeked around the door to find Robert Upchurch standing there, all dressed up in a baby blue tuxedo. He looked like one of those skinny blue Popsicles you get from the ice-cream truck, only with a ruffled shirt and a bow tie.

"Don't tell me, Robert. It's Halloween, and you're trying on your Dork Man costume," I said.

"For your information, Hank, I'm rehearsing."

"He's trying out to be the little man on top of a wedding cake," Frankie said. We all cracked up.

"Very funny." Robert snorted with his goofy laugh that sounds like a hyena with a cold. "Actually, I am practicing to be an emcee."

Emily walked into the clubhouse, uninvited as usual.

"Robert has been selected as the master of

ceremonies for the Parade of Athletes," she said.

"Selected!" Frankie laughed. "Nobody else applied for the job."

"Robert, just do your routine," Ashley said.

"Wait a minute," I said. "I thought we were having a meeting."

"The meeting has been postponed," Ashley said. "Robert needs to try out his opening remarks for tomorrow night on us."

"This I have to see," I said, hurling myself across the room to the couch and landing half on the arm and half on the pillow—which, I might add, didn't feel too good on the old tush area.

"Excuse me," Emily said. "Is anyone going to move over and make room for me?"

Emily is as skinny as Robert is, so she doesn't take up much space. I scrunched up on the couch and got as comfortable as a guy can be who's sitting arm to arm with his little sister.

"Hit it, Robert," Frankie said. "Do your stuff."

Robert cleared his throat.

"Good evening, ladies and gentleman.

Welcome to the Parade of Athletes. The word *athlete* derives from the ancient Greek and Latin words used to refer to someone who competed in public games. The earliest use of the word can be traced to—"

"Cut!" Ashley called out.

"What's wrong?" Robert asked.

"Everything, dude!" Frankie said. "I'm already asleep and the show hasn't even started."

"I thought it was fascinating information," Robert said.

"Yeah, if you're writing an encyclopedia," Ashley said. "The people tomorrow night are coming to see sports, not to hear a lecture."

"Maybe I'll lead off with a joke, then," Robert said. "Actually, I have several highly entertaining ones."

"We'll be the judge of that," Frankie said.

"Here goes. Why is it so hot after a soccer game?"

"Why?" I called out.

"Because all the fans have gone home."

Robert did his congested hyena laugh, and Emily burst into hysterics like she had just seen a naked clown. We just sat there with our jaws hanging open.

"Maybe you should start and end with 'good evening, ladies and gentlemen,' " Frankie said. "You do that really well."

"I do?" Robert asked. "Do you really think so?"

We all agreed because we didn't want to have to listen to another one of his jokes.

"Wow," Robert said, "I never knew five words could be so powerful."

He spun on his heels, and walked out the door and down the hall toward the elevator. As he walked, we could hear him repeating those words, over and over, in all kinds of different voices.

"Good evening, ladies and gentlemen," he said, sounding like an English actor in one of those old movies my dad watches.

"Gentlemen and ladies, good evening," he said, sounding like Robert's version of a hip-hop deejay—which, trust me, he will never ever be.

My sister, Emily, ran after him like a puppy dog following a bouncing ball. "Robert, however you say it, it sounds so dreamy," she said.

We were quiet until we heard them get in the elevator. Then we burst out laughing.

"Do we want to talk about what just happened?" Ashley asked.

"There are no words that come to my mind," Frankie said. "For the first time in my life, I am speechless."

"Good," I said, "because I have something important to tell you guys."

"Like where you've been for the last ten days," Frankie said.

"As a matter of fact, yeah."

"So?" Frankie said. "Spill it, Zip."

"I've been playing a new sport."

"Does it involve a ball?" Ashley asked, starting to twirl her ponytail around her finger like she does when she's thinking. She loves guessing games.

"Sure."

"Which one?" said Frankie. "Base, foot, soft, basket?"

"Not exactly any of those. A different kind of ball—white and smaller."

"Golf!" Frankie said, and held up his hand to high-five me. "I've always wanted to hit a long drive like Tiger Woods. Where have you been playing?"

"Not on a golf course. Because it's not golf."

"A small, white ball," Ashley said, thinking out loud. "Not on a golf course. Can I ask you—is it lighter than a golf ball?"

"Yup."

Ashley broke out into a huge smile. "Ping-Pong!" she yelled. "You're playing Ping-Pong!"

"Yes, I am, but could you keep your voice down about it? I don't want the whole building to know."

"Why? What's the big whoop?" Frankie asked.

"Well, you know. Ping-Pong isn't exactly respected by the athletic community."

"Zip, where'd you get that piece of info?" Frankie said.

"My dad told me."

"I don't mean to be disrespectful, but Stan the Man's eyes are crossed."

"You said it yourself, Frankie, that day on the yard with McKelty. Ping-Pong is a wimpy sport."

"Zip, my man. I never said that."

"You compared it to your aunt Eleanor playing shuffleboard."

"Last I checked, you're not my aunt Eleanor. I'm sure a paddle looks very different in your hands, Hank Man."

"Are you going to demonstrate Ping-Pong tomorrow night at the Parade of Athletes?" Ashley asked.

"No way! Nick McKelty will take me apart piece by piece."

"Who cares what that moron thinks?" Frankie said. "If he thinks at all."

"Yeah, he's just a snaggletoothed idiot," Ashley agreed.

"I hear he's doing some really cool soccer drills at the Parade of Athletes," I said. "Like dribbling through cones with his hands tied behind his back."

"You don't *need* your hands in soccer," Ashley said. "McKelty just comes up with things to make himself look cooler than he is."

"Yeah, you've got more talent than he does in your two front teeth."

"True, I *am* good at chewing," I said. Frankie and Ashley cracked up at that, and I did too.

"Anyway, do me a favor, guys," I said. "Let's keep my Ping-Pong career just between us. I really don't want McKelty to know."

"For how long?" Ashley asked.

"Until I say you can say," I said.

We put our hands out in front of us, one on top of the other, and yelled out "Magik 3" to seal the deal. That's the name of our magic act that we've had for over a year now. We take our Magik 3 oaths very seriously.

It was getting late, and we all had homework to finish. Actually, I had homework to *start* and finish. Because of my learning challenges, I'm not exactly fast in the homework department. Or in any department involving books, paper, pencils, erasers, words, letters, or numbers. I could go on, but I think you get the idea.

We left the clubhouse and hurried to the elevator.

"Hey, Hank," Ashley whispered as she pushed the up button. "Do you think it will be longer than a month? I've never kept a secret more than thirty-one days."

"Hard to say, Ash," I answered. "But I'm counting on you."

The elevator door opened, and my mom came out carrying a basket of dirty clothes to take to the laundry room down the hall. Cheerio was with her. When he saw me, he came running over and let a Ping-Pong ball drop out of his mouth in front of my feet. It rolled down the hall, clicking and clacking as it bounced along the linoleum floor.

"Ashley and I are cool with your secret," Frankie said. "But it looks like your dog's a blabbermouth."

Cheerio wagged his tail and started running in circles. He may not be able to keep a secret, but he sure is cute.

CHAPTER 24

"GOOD EVENING, LADIES AND GENTLEMEN," Robert said, clutching the microphone in his bony little fingers. "Welcome to the Parade of Athletes."

He was holding the mike so tight that you could see his white knuckles all the way in the bleachers, where my mom and dad and Papa Pete and I were sitting.

Our gym was packed with parents, teachers, aunts, uncles, older sisters, younger brothers— all there to cheer on their favorite athlete. The kids who were participating were warming up on the gym floor, wearing shorts and blue and green T-shirts that said PS 87. I, on the other hand, was sitting in between my mom and dad, not warming up, and not wearing athletic clothes.

Wait. I do have on my Mets sweatshirt. I wonder if that counts?

I have to admit, I was feeling pretty bad about my decision not to participate in the Parade of Athletes. I just couldn't risk the embarrassment of showing my lousy hand-eye, hand-foot, foot-knee, eye-elbow coordination to everyone.

Papa Pete leaned across my mom and put his big hand on my knee. "Hankie, there's Sam Chin warming up with his dad," he said. "Maybe it's not too late for you to sign up for the Ping-Pong demonstration."

"Papa Pete! Please! Don't say the P. P. word in public."

"What's wrong with saying Ping-Pong? Hankie, I was just trying to . . ."

Before he could finish, he was drowned out by Robert tapping on the microphone.

"Good evening, ladies and gentlemen," he repeated. "I'd like to start the festivities with a little joke."

No, Robert! Don't do it! Don't do it!

"I've selected a joke with a sporting theme," Robert said.

"Just do the joke already, idiot!" McKelty yelled from his place on the floor where he was warming up for his soccer drill.

"Okay, here goes," Robert said. "Why can't you play basketball with pigs?"

"Because they stink, like you!" McKelty yelled. No one laughed but him.

McKelty's dad got up from the stands, went over to Nick, and had a little heart-to-heart with him.

Good. It's time somebody put that jerk in his place.

"The reason you can't play basketball with pigs," Robert said, "is because they HOG the ball."

The only person who laughed was my sister Emily. The rest of the people in the gym were dead silent. If I were Robert, I would have run away to Mongolia to live with wild camels and never come back to PS 87. But not Robert. He hung in there.

"Maybe you didn't get it," he said. "I can do it again."

"Thank you, that will be quite enough, Robert," I heard Ms. Adolf say.

Where was she? I didn't see her anywhere. And then I did.

Oh, my crazy eyes, tell me I'm not seeing what I'm seeing.

But I was. There was Ms. Adolf, all decked out in her fencing gear. No joke. She had on a jacket that looked like a bulletproof vest (it was grey, of course), a full mask with a mesh face that looked like a screen door, short pants with buttons at the knees, and tights like George Washington always wore in pictures. And she was carrying a long silver sword. She looked like Blackbeard the Pirate. Except she was in grey and didn't have a beard, so I guess she looked like Grey Bun the Pirate.

"To begin the festivities, I am about to give a brief display of my advance-and-retreat thrusting technique," Ms. Adolf said through her screen-door mask.

"You go, girlfriend," I heard Frankie call out.

"Without further ado, I will demonstrate the lunge, the thrust, and the parry," she said.

And without further ado, whatever ado is, she leaped onto the rubber mat that ran alongside the bleachers and starting lunging forward, forward, forward—then retreating backward, backward, backward. She looked like a crazed musketeer.

"Wow," Papa Pete said. "She's got some command of the blade. Is she married?"

"Are you kidding, Papa Pete?" I said, whipping my head in his direction so fast, it nearly took off.

"Yes, I am."

"Thank goodness. You scared me for a minute."

When she was all thrust out, Ms. Adolf pulled off her mask, held it under her arm, and saluted the crowd with her sword. "Thank you, friends of the foil," she said.

The audience sat there in silence at first, then Papa Pete started to applaud. Soon, everyone joined in, and Ms. Adolf took another bow. As quickly as she was up, she was down—back on the bench reserved for the teachers.

Before anyone could stop him, Robert grabbed the microphone again. "Maybe I should present another comedy moment," he suggested.

"No!" all the kids shouted.

"All right, then, I'll save it for after intermission." Boy, that Robert. He doesn't take a hint.

After that, the evening really took off. There

was equipment of all kinds spread out over the gym floor: a trampoline, a line of soccer cones and a goal net, a portable basketball hoop, a pommel horse and a mat for gymnastics and karate. Two rings and a long rope hung from the ceiling.

I noticed that a Ping-Pong table had been set up right in the middle of the gym floor. Just looking at it made me itch to play, but I was determined not to. Any Ping-Pong embarrassment was going to be between me and my pals at the Ping-Pong Emporium.

The Parade of Athletes began. Christopher Hook did backflips, front flips, seat drops, and a fantastic double twist on the trampoline. He was terrific for a third-grader. Actually, he was terrific for an any-grader.

A lot of kids shot baskets. A whole team of girls did a slam-dunk demonstration on one of those toy plastic basketball hoops. The big surprise during the fifth-grade demonstration was Heather Payne, who turned out to be a short, blond, girl-type version of Michael Jordan. I mean, wow, she had a sky hook. Who would've guessed that underneath all that perfect penmanship and straight As there was a hoop star waiting to be born.

Another huge surprise was that Joelle Adwin was able to detach herself from her cell phone long enough to actually do a gymnastics routine. At least, I think that's what it was. The official name of what she did is rhythmic gymnastics. It involves a stick with colorful ribbons tied to it and a lot of hopping around on the mat.

To be totally honest, it didn't look like a real sport to me. But since I *know* that's exactly how a lot of people feel about Ping-Pong, and since I *know* it is a truly difficult sport, I decided to give Joelle all the credit she deserved. When she twirled her last twirl, I stood up and applauded until my hands tingled. Even McKelty turned around and gave me a look like I had lost my mind.

That's okay, Mister. You wouldn't understand us athletes who choose unusual sports.

"In case anyone is wondering, which I'm sure you are," Joelle said when the applause had died down, "I designed this costume myself. It's called Black of Night with Red Flower."

And in case you're wondering, which I'm

sure you're not, it was a black leotard with a red flower on it.

I was amazed to see how many kids were good at some sport. Sarah Stern actually had a black belt in karate, which I think is excellent for a third-grader. Even Katie Sperling and Kim Paulson were impressive as they wrapped their legs around the climbing rope and shot to the ceiling to ring the bell. And Luke Whitman got his fingers out of his nose long enough to grab the rings and do an Iron Cross. You have to be pretty strong to pull that off.

"Look over there, Hankie," Papa Pete said, tapping my hand again to get my attention. "Sam Chin is getting ready to play."

I looked at the Ping-Pong table and saw Sam's dad, Winston, setting up a box for him to stand on. Sam was taking his paddle out of his case. He didn't look too happy. As a matter of fact, he looked downright scared.

I felt a little hand pulling at my shirt. "Hi, Hank. It's me."

"Mason!" I said. "You're supposed to be down there, doing your soccer demonstration."

"My mommy says it's after the inter-something. I forget the word."

"Intermission."

"Yeah, that word. Bye."

He ran off and went back to his mother, who was sitting in the front row next to Sam Chin's mom. Mason made me smile. Every time I get to help him learn something, no matter how small—even if it's just a word—it makes me feel great.

I turned back to the gym floor. Frankie and Ashley and the other jock soccer players were kicking the ball around the cones, warming up for the dribbling and kicking and passing demonstrations.

"That's what you should be doing, Hank," my dad said, pointing to them. "I still can't understand why you didn't sign up for tonight."

"Let him be, Stan," my mom whispered.

I ask you, where would we kids be without moms?

By now, Sam was standing on his box and Winston Chin had taken his place at the other side of the Ping-Pong table. He was going to rally with Sam.

Okay, serve it up, Sam. Show them how the game is played.

But Sam just stood there, holding his paddle in one hand and the ball in the other. He looked out at all the people watching him, and I thought he was going to cry. He father went over to him and kneeled down to say something, but I couldn't make out what he was saying.

"Come on, you baby. It's only Ping-Pong," a voice shouted from the front row of the bleachers.

I'll bet you can guess whose voice it was. You're right. Who else but Nick the Tick McKelty would harass a cute little kid who was scared to death?

Sam Chin looked over at McKelty. I could see his face start to scrunch up. He was trying hard not to cry. McKelty cupped his hands over his erupting volcano of a mouth.

"Hurry up, kid. No one wants to see Ping-Pong, anyway."

Ms. Adolf got up and walked over to McKelty. She looked mad, and for the first time in my life, I was on her side.

Sam Chin couldn't hold it in anymore. When

he heard McKelty's nasty remark, he burst into tears, jumped off his box, and ran to his mom's arms like a little duckling swimming to his mommy duck.

"Come with me," Ms. Adolf said to McKelty. "Your evening is over."

"You can't do that," he answered her. "I'm a key man in the soccer demonstration."

"Not tonight, you aren't. This is the Parade of Athletes. A true athlete possesses good sportsmanship. Now parade yourself right out of the gymnasium."

There is no messing with Ms. Adolf when she gets that tone of voice. McKelty got up and shuffled out of the gym. We all cheered, every single one of us. Sam Chin didn't care that McKelty was gone. He was still sitting with his face buried in his mom's neck. Poor little guy.

Mr. Rock picked up the microphone for an announcement. He's so nice, I'm sure he didn't want everyone to be staring at Sam.

"I'm afraid we'll have to postpone the Ping-Pong demonstration for another evening," he said.

"Unless there's someone else who'd like to

show us his Ping-Pong moves," said a voice from the floor. It was Ashley.

Ashweena, we talked about this. DON'T YOU DARE.

"Maybe there's another person here who's really good at Ping-Pong," she went on. "Like, say, one of the fifth-graders."

"Ashley, do you have someone specific in mind?" Mr. Rock asked her.

She looked up at me without moving her eyes. I shook my head at her without moving my head. When you've been close friends for as long as we have, you know how to communicate without saying a word or without making a move.

I knew that she knew the answer was no.

I wasn't playing any public Ping-Pong. And that's all there was to it.

CHAPTER 25

AFTER INTERMISSION, it was soccer time. The little kids went up first. Mason did a kicking-for-accuracy drill that would have blown your mind. That little guy kicked twenty power shots right into the net: ten with his left foot and ten with his right. Not many five-year-olds can do that *and* draw a perfect Brooklyn Bridge in the sandbox, I can tell you that.

When he was done, I jumped to my feet and whistled. "Atta boy, Mason!" I hollered.

"Come down here, Hank!" he shouted. "It's fun."

"The child has a point," Papa Pete whispered to me. "Fun is fun."

"We've already gone over this, Papa Pete. No, no, and no."

Mason went over and sat down next to his mom in the front row. Sam Chin was still there.

He wasn't exactly buried in his mom's neck anymore, but he was still clinging pretty hard to her.

I wondered if he was going to remember this night for the rest of his life. Probably. You never forget the really embarrassing moments. I still shudder remembering the night I burst out crying in the kindergarten talent show singing "This Land Is Your Land." I ran into the coat closet and didn't come out until everyone else had gone home.

By the time Ashley and Frankie got up to do their demonstration, everyone was ready to see something spectacular. Let's face it. Who doesn't love to watch a great soccer player? They're fast and skillful and light on their feet. And, I have to tell you, two of the best ever are my good buddies, Frankie Townsend and Ashley Wong.

Ashley did a kicking demonstration that was awesome. She set up five basketballs so each one was balanced on an orange cone of a different height. Then she kicked the soccer ball at each cone. If she hit it squarely, she'd knock the basketball down. If she didn't, the basketball would remain on the cone.

"First, I'll kick from fifteen feet away," she announced to the crowd.

She did, and she knocked down all five basketballs, one after another.

"Now I'll kick from thirty feet away," she said.

"Impossible," whispered my dad.

"Show them, Ashweena," I called out. She gave me a thumbs-up and took aim. I held my breath as she kicked. One, two, three, four, five. All five basketballs went flying off their cones.

Next it was Frankie's turn. He was demonstrating his dribbling and passing technique. First he dribbled around a long row of cones in less than ten seconds, ending with a perfect pass to Ashley. Then he did the same thing, but this time he dribbled only with his right foot. Do you have any idea how hard that is?

For his grand finale, he dribbled around the row of cones using only his left foot, and he finished off with a perfect aereial shot into the goal net.

Talk about your standing ovations! Everyone was on their feet. I was jumping around so much that I almost didn't feel the little hand tugging on the back of my shirt.

I thought it was Mason again, but it wasn't. It was Sam Chin. "I'll play if you'll play," he said to me.

"What?" I asked. It was hard to hear him with all the noise. I bent down closer. "What are you talking about, Sam?"

"I got scared. Mason said you're scared too. Maybe we won't be so scared together."

Oh, wow. This is big.

I knew how important it was for Sam to go back onto the floor and play. I always wished that I had come out of the cloakroom and finished my song way back in kindergarten. At least I would have known that I could do it. To this very day, when I hear "This Land Is Your Land," I get sick to my stomach.

"You're a big boy, Sam. You can go by yourself and play with your dad."

"No, I can't."

Sam Chin gave my hand a tug. "Let's play Ping-Pong, Hank. You're good."

I looked over at Papa Pete. I looked at that room full of people. I looked at the double doors to the gym and saw Nick McKelty's eyes peering into the room, watching everything that was going on.

I looked at Sam Chin. How could I say no to that face? "Sure, why not?" I said.

CHAPTER 26

PING! SAM CHIN HIT A FAST SERVE down the middle of the table.

Pong. I returned it, smooth as glass.

Ping! Sam sent me a topspin return.

Pong! I answered it with my own backhand spin.

We rallied for five minutes in that gym. Back and forth, steady and even, in a rhythmic groove. Sam standing on his box, me bouncing in my Nikes. When we finished, everyone in the gym was on their feet, clapping.

Sam turned to the crowd and took absolutely, positively the cutest bow you've ever seen. That kid had a smile on his face that was as big as the sun. When he ran to his mom, this time he didn't bury his face in her neck. Nope. This time, he pumped his arms over his head and danced around like a wild man.

Way to go, Sam Chin, I thought as I waved at the crowd and hummed a little bit of "This Land Is Your Land."

"L you want to show them some of your moves?" Winston Chin said to me over the roar of the crowd.

"I wouldn't mind showing *him* a thing or two," I said, looking toward the door, where a certain large, snaggletoothed, bad-breathed bully was still looking in.

"Just remember the Three Cs," Winston said. "Concentrate. Control. Confidence."

The crowd got quiet as he picked up a paddle and went to his side of the table and I took my side. He served the first ball. It came fast, cutting a wide angle across the table. *Concentrate, Hank.* I took a big lunge and hit a looping return shot.

Ping!

"That's it, Hank," Winston said. "The reflexes of the bobcat."

He fired another shot at me. His shots only came in three speeds: fast, really fast, and faster than that. *Control, Hank.* I wanted to slam it, but I knew if I did, it would fly off the table. So

I took a breath, then raced to the ball and held out my paddle to block it.

Pong!

"Good, Hank," Winston said. "The speed of the cheetah."

The next ball came at me with so much back-spin, it looked like it was going in two directions at once. *Confidence, Hank.* I knew I had to wait for the ball, to follow its twisting path before hitting it. I crouched, waited, then returned it with my own special backspin.

Ping!

"Yes, Hank," Winston said. "The craftiness of the fox!"

Let me just say—and I really, really don't mean to brag—it was the best match I'd ever played in my whole life.

Everyone at the Parade of Athletes that night had a great time watching us play, but I'll be straight with you. The one who had the best time of all was me.

When the match was over, a lot of the people in the gym crowded around me, cheering like I was a star athlete or something.

"Hank, you're a Ping-Pong wizard," Ashley

said, throwing her arms around me.

"Where'd you learn to do that, dude?" Frankie asked.

"Here and there," I said, smiling.

"Wow, you're good, Zip."

"I could improve."

"Right, and my name's Bernice."

My mom and dad and Papa Pete came down from the bleachers to slap me on the back and shake my hand and hug me all at once.

"I'm so proud of you, honey," my mom said.

"Me too," my dad said. "You played very well, son. Ping-Pong is quite a sport."

Wait a minute. Did he say sport? Yes, he did. Stan Zipzer, I think you're trying to tell me something.

"Dad," I said, "does this mean that now I can finally quit soccer?"

"Like I've always said, Hank, I think concentrating on one sport is a fine way to go."

That was close enough for me! I started to cheer too.

So long, Coach Gilroy. I won't be taking a knee for your team anymore!

So long, Game Face. I won't be needing you anymore, either!

Papa Pete could see how happy I was. He threw his big hairy arm around me and shook my shoulder like I was a teddy bear.

"What does everyone say to a root-beer float?" he said. "On me."

"I say that sounds great," I answered at the top of my lungs. I was so happy to be part of the Parade of Athletes, after all. And to think I almost didn't let myself be part of this great moment. I'll never do a thing like that again.

As we all walked out of the gym—my mom and dad, Frankie and Ashley, Emily and Robert and Papa Pete—I saw Nick McKelty standing in the hall by himself.

"Hey, Zipzer," he said.

"Yeah?"

He looked at me a long time. Then he spoke.

I'll bet you think that big lug congratulated me for playing a great game. Well, you're wrong.

"I still think Ping-Pong's for subhumans," he said.

"That's *your* problem, McKelty," I said.

And together with my family and friends, we went out to celebrate that I finally found the right sport for me.